Melissa Chan has lived in Europe, the United States of America, and (briefly) China. After growing up in the Western Australian wheatbelt, she moved to the Eastern seaboard where she works as a lawyer. Her fiction has appeared in *Ita, Womanspeak* and *Angels of Power and other reproductive creations*, the first Spinifex Press anthology. *Too Rich*, a murder mystery novel featuring the lesbian film critic and detective, Francesca Miles, was published by Spinifex Press in 1991.

Other books by Melissa Chan:
Too Rich

GETTING YOUR MAN

Melissa Chan

SPINIFEX PRESS
Australia

Spinifex Press Pty Ltd,
504 Queensberry Street,
North Melbourne, Vic. 3051
Australia

First published by Spinifex Press, 1992

Typeset in 10/12 pt Times extended 105%
        by Lorna Hendry, Melbourne
Production by Sylvana Scannapiego,
        Island Graphics, Melbourne
Made and Printed in Australia by The Book Printer, Victoria
Cover design: Liz Nicholson – Design BITE
The contents of this book have been printed
        on 100% recycled paper

National Library of Australia
Cataloguing-in-Publication entry:
CIP
Chan, Melissa, 1947–
    Getting your man.

    ISBN 1-875559-08-6

    1. Title.

A823.3

Contents

Piecework

SYLVIA DOBROSKA AND Drina Hussein agreed they were sick and tired of it. Sick and tired of the hard work and little pay that working day and night on machines, sewing hems and seams and tucks, making whole garments, struggling with tough men's overall material one day, delicate lingerie the next, brought them. For two years they had been slaves, virtual slaves, to the treadle. No spanking brand new electric sewing machines for them. In the world of the outworker, the woman working long hours, for low pay, in the privacy (or prison) of her own home, "all mod cons" did not apply. Nor did industrial health and safety regulations, rules that factories and shops had to pretend they were living up to. No insurance in the piece-work industry. No superannuation. No longservice leave. No overaward payments; indeed, no award payments. Despite the work of the trade union movement in securing an award, and their vigilance in the industry, too many middlemen escaped. There were no margins for skill: no middleman would think of it, let alone countenance paying any extra. And no extra pay-ments for boredom, repetitive work, feelings of being cooped up in a workhouse. No danger money, though sewing machines can be dangerous.

Drina had run a needle right through her finger once. The finger hung there, needle showing in one side and out the other. Stunned, she had sat, skewered, until she had realised that if she didn't get the needle out, no one else would. Gingerly, Drina had eased her finger down the slim steel spike, over the pointed end, and off. Tetanus? She had taken out her bicycle and ridden over to the local hospital for an injection, just in

1

case. Her sister had had a friend who died of lock-jaw after jabbing her finger with an ordinary sewing needle and going out to work in the garden, amongst the bulbs and weeds and manure. Drina loved life, despite its present drudgery.

Renda Piliavin, further down the street, was sick of piecework too. So was Marian Bubek. And Maria Trevaskis. And Zussana Helm. And now, each knew the other felt the same: the tiredness, the boredom, the numb fingers, the cramped leg muscles, aching shoulders and neck. And the "middleman" making money out of them and their daily grind. They had come to the end of the road. It was time for action.

Two years ago, Sylvia Dobroska was approached by Mr Sampson at the supermarket. He had asked her if she would like to take in sewing. She had jumped at the chance. Who wouldn't, in her situation: newly arrived from Rumania, little English, fourteen-year-old daughter, no husband, no job. She didn't even ask how much it paid. And when she found out it was $3.50 an item (or sometimes $2.00 for smaller articles) she didn't question him. Just took it, grateful for what she could get.

In those first months, Sylvia thought Mr Sampson was doing her a favour. She hadn't questioned his bringing her the sewing, then taking away the finished garments, and selling them for more, far more, than he ever paid to her. She hadn't really known how much more. She hadn't understood the ways of the middleman, the man who picks up the work from the factories, delivers it to the homeworkers, then collects it and returns it, for a handsome profit.

So grateful had she been, so excited at earning money for the first time, that she had run down the street, knocking at the doors of the few women she knew, telling them of her good fortune. She had wanted to pass her good luck to them. The next week, when Mr Sampson brought her a load of material, cut into patterns, for sewing, she had timidly asked him if he wanted more work, more workers. He had acted standoffish, at first. Answered her brusquely. Told her it was tight times, there was little work about, that she had better concentrate on her own industry, without worrying about others. She had been quite scared. Afraid he would forget her, strike her off his list, and she would lose his benevolence as quickly as she had gained it. All night, Sylvia sat up worrying, working harder and harder at her machine, treadling until her legs cramped right there on the spot. But two days later he had come by to collect what she had done. After marking the garments off on the page on the clip board he carried with him, he had casually asked her about her friends.

"They'd like to make some money too, would they? Do some work for me?" he asked. "Yes," she had replied, eagerly. "Got machines of their own?" he returned. "Yes," she had said, nodding vigorously, willing to please, wanting to get them his help.

He had asked her to tell them he'd call on each of them, individually, the following week, between 10.00 AM and 11.00. Immediately he left, she had rushed out of the house, knocking at Drina Hussein's door, just three houses down. Then the two of them had hurried out to see Renda Piliavin, four doors away, on the other side of the street. Renda had put on the kettle, while Sylvia ran out the back door and skipped through the brokendown fence, knocking at Marian Bubek's kitchen window when she saw her working at the sink. They had gone together, next door, to Zussana Helm. And Drina had run around the corner to Maria Trevaskis, dragging her away from making the beds, so she could join them in a kitchen table discussion about this new possibility.

For eighteen months they had worked away industriously, scarcely coming out of their homes to meet, quickly going about their housework, so time was free to work at their machines. They had organised their shopping according to a roster, by the calendar month, so that one week Sylvia and Drina went to the supermarket and the greengrocer for the six of them; the next week Drina did the weekly shopping for them all, with Marian Bubek. The third week, it was Marian and Zussana Helm's turn. The week after, Zussana joined Renda Piliavin. The fifth week, Maria Trevaskis and Renda took the trolleys and loaded them up, selecting the items from the shelves and the display cases with a professionalism born of the need to be thrifty – and quick: there was always work waiting for them at their machines; there was always more where that work came from.

Mr Sampson had kept up the flow of overalls and lingerie, collars and cuffs, shirts and trousers. Slacks had been added, as had been workcaps, on which Sylvia had broken many a nail and Renda had sobbed in frustration until Maria had shown each of them the easiest way to do an impossible job. "Take it around, gently, like this," she said, indicating on her machine how she slipped the material under the foot, then flipped it around at just the right point, and manoeuvred the curve of the brim so that it fitted flush against the rounded edge of the cap.

As the work came, and continued to come, they celebrated their good fortune. Inwardly, each was gleeful at the money added to their tightly stretched budgets. Outwardly, they rejoiced together, at brief coffee mornings they arranged when whose ever turn it was to do the shopping came to collect the money, or to return the goods. Never did they imagine Mr Sampson was profiting rudely from their industry. At least, not until some eighteen or more months after the shopping roster began. And they learned it purely by chance.

One Wednesday morning, piecework pickup time from the Footscray area, Sylvia Dobroska had worked with such concentration over the past week that Mr Sampson couldn't carry all the garments out to his van, parked in the street. Sylvia had offered to help, making a journey out to the kerb, her arms piled high. Placing the pile gently, but securely, into the back of the vehicle, she noticed Mr Sampson's clipboard. Usually, he had it under his arm, or in his hand. It was almost as if it were attached to his body, an extension of his limbs, or a fixture on the underarm of his jacket or coat.

Glancing idly down at it, almost unaware that her eyes were methodically taking in the content of what was written there, Sylvia observed columns of figures next to names which ran down the left hand margin, with company names written along the top of the page.

"Renda Piliavin", she read. "Drina Hussein." "Maria Trevaskis." "Sylvia Dobroska..." Then along the top: "Regent Bar Overalls, Inc." "Sissoons Lingerie, Pty. Ltd." "Trudy Danielle – Ladies' Lights Inc." "Warners Workcaps, Ltd." But it was the figures, carefully written in the inside columns of the grid, that made her gasp. "Overalls: 30 pieces @ $30.00." "Petties: 45 pieces @ $20.00." "Workcaps: 49 pieces @ $10.00."

She looked again, harder, disbelieving. It was true. Garments she and Renda and Drina and Marian and Zussana and Maria worked hours to complete, for $3.50 an item, or $2.00 for the caps, sold back to the companies at ten times the price they were paid. Surely she was seeing double. The figures must be wrong. It must be a mistake. She looked again. It was true. Looking up, she saw Mr Sampson coming back down the path, his arms full. Hastily, she pushed the clipboard to one side, so that it would not be evident to him that she had seen it, and adjusted the pile of clothes in the van.

"This is the last lot, I managed to get it all into one pile," said Mr Sampson, unaware that he had just been disclosed, to one of his hardest workers, one of his most grateful outwork "team", as the sweatshop tyrant. One of his *once* most grateful team members, thought Sylvia.

"I'll just put them in, next to that lot, then everything's set." He deposited the garments in the nearest available spot, then leant over to pick up his clipboard from where Sylvia had pushed it, several arms' lengths from where she was now standing.

"Next Friday, then," he said.

He had decided to come back twice a week, now, since she was getting so much done. Although he hadn't put it quite like that. Rather, told her the companies were getting anxious about the work, and were wanting it done faster and faster, just so she would be worried about her job, and work harder and harder. She saw it now. The aim was to make more money for him, and the urgency with which he spoke of the demands of the companies was an urgency he felt, for more work, more garments finished, more sweat, more money – for him.

As he drove a short distance down the street, stopping midway between Drina Hussein and Renda Piliavin's houses, Sylvia stood, looking after the van. This was terrible. She had not realised such a thing could happen in Australia, where she had been taught there was a fair day's pay for a fair day's work. That was what she had read in the leaflets and letters they had sent her when she had written to the authorities in Budapest, enquiring about emigrating. She had believed it. She still believed it. But she also believed her own eyes. The figures she had seen on the clipboard couldn't be wrong. Or could they? Surely Mr Sampson knew his business? Unfortunately, it seemed, Mr Sampson knew his business far better than she knew hers – or Renda, or Maria, or Zussana or the others knew theirs. And she was responsible. She had got them into it. She would have to think of some way of getting them out of it, or, better still, evening up the returns. Why should they do all the work, and Mr Sampson make all the profit?

Maria Trevaskis had always been good at figures. She thrived on the atmosphere at Footscray College of Technical and Further Education. She found going over the lessons each week with Sylvia Dobroska, exhilarating. Every Thursday evening, promptly at 5.30 PM, the two of them rode on their bicycles to Footscray TAFE, their books and papers perched securely in wire baskets attached to the handlebars. Renda, Marian, Zussana and Drina took turns at "babysitting": looking after Lucilla, Sylvia's daughter, and Maria's two, Trinca and Joseph.

In the last few months Renda had been putting in most time with the children on Thursday nights: the classes ran for three hours and Maria and Sylvia were there, often until well after nine o'clock. Renda's two eldest, Sammy and Josepha, had left home some years before, starting their own families in Ringwood and Forest Hill. They lived so far away, she rarely went to visit them and her grandchildren. Even more rarely did they come to visit her. "It's too far, mother," Josepha would complain. "And we've got to do things around the house on weekends." "It's such a long drive, Mum," echoed Sammy, his eyes fixed on the television screen whenever she had managed to get out there herself, taking her bicycle with her in the train and cycling the quarter mile from the station.

Renda was pleased her children had moved up in the world, although she was saddened that her grandchildren were growing up away from their grandmother. Then Georgio, her "baby" had left home, too. Now, she had the house all to herself. She welcomed Lucilla and Trinca and Joseph, caring for them as if they were her own. And they enjoyed her company.

The life of a single parent had been hard: Renda had come to Australia with her husband in 1971. He had worked first for Horgon's, in the meatworks, and had come home smelling of meat. Long baths had done little to remove the clinging smell, and it began to invade the house, too. He left Horgon's, worked for Ford Motor Company, then General Motors Holden. Then he got a job in the building industry. One day, one of his workmates came to her with the news. He had fallen off the scaffolding at one of the building sites. She was a widow, with three children growing up. She learned about the widow's pension from a neighbour, and began struggling to keep herself and the children on social security, supplemented by odd jobs here and there. She had worked as a nightpacker in the local supermarket for some years, concerned about leaving the children at home alone, but needing the extra few dollars packing tins and bread and biscuits, cheese, meat and eggs, on to the supermarket shelves and into the display cabinets. Then in swift succession Sammy and Josepha had left. She had begun taking on piecework with the others. Now, with Georgio gone, too, in her empty house, she looked forward to Thursday nights babysitting.

The TAFE course had been Sylvia's idea. She had produced a worn copy of the *Age* when they had sat down together, that terrible day she had realised how badly she and the others were being paid, and how grandly Mr Sampson was living as a result.

"Look, friends," she had said, spreading the article on Renda's kitchen table and pointing at the caption written under the title BIG BUSINESS:

7

"Women today are the prime movers in the establishment of small businesses. Fiona Athersmith and Michael Fitzgerald speak to the women who have moved away from traditional employment roles to step out on their own."

One of the women in the article had set up a small business with her husband, and to make it run effectively had attended the Preston TAFE Small Business Centre. It had given her advice on how to structure a business, to establish records and cash flow, and how to plan for a profit. She had learned how to improve her business skills, and how to go about marketing.

"This is what we've got to do," announced Sylvia. Maria nodded her head vigorously. "I'd like that," she said, shyly. She had felt embarrassed about her maths ability when she was at school. She always seemed to come top, and it was not long before she realised that this did not please the teachers, or the boys. Girls just were not supposed to be "good" at arithmetic. When she received top marks, she knew she had "done the wrong thing". For a long time she couldn't understand it. She really could not understand it, even now. She had begun to pretend she was unable to follow the teacher's instructions. And before long, she was coming near the bottom of the class. At home, she had studied her homework and her maths book, completing the exercises without any errors. But the work she took to school brought her low marks, and she deliberately began failing in her examinations. Now, she saw a chance to redeem herself. Maybe others might not like her being able to add up three columns of figures at once, but she was secretly proud of it. And she wanted to learn more.

That day, they agreed to set up a fund, together, to pay for the books and stationery, and any fees, for Sylvia Dobroska and Maria Trevaskis to take whatever accounting or business courses were available at the local TAFE. Sylvia and Maria went down the next day to look at the brochures. They selected a course on "Accounting for Small Business", and paid their enrolment fees at once.

But the others were eager to join in the enterprise. How could they help in escaping the clutches of Mr Sampson and the piecework trade? All very well to have accounting skills and business knowledge, but in the end you had to get the work from somewhere. They knew Mr Sampson must have worked over the years to build up his contacts with the companies whose work they did. They had no knowledge of the industry, apart from their own hard work in it. They needed to know the names of the businesses taking their work from Mr Sampson, and giving him the material, cut to the patterns they sewed and sweated over on their machines. More than this, if they were to run their own business – they hardly dared think they might – they would have to build up contacts. They would have to gain the confidence of the company managers, or at least the people down the line who parcelled out the work to middlemen like Mr Sampson. They would have to get orders for work to be done. They would have to assure the companies they could perform the work, and that they had sufficient hands and machines to get the garments sewn. Perfectly. As soon as needed. No delays. No mess ups. No problems with the piece workers. Everyone kept in line.

Drina Hussein put herself forward. "I can do it," she said, a little haltingly at first, embarrassed by her own assertions about her abilities. She went on, growing more confident as she spoke.

"We've just got to find out which companies Mr Sampson uses, then work out how to approach them, and how to convince them we can produce the goods. But we've been working for ages in the industry without any complaints from Mr Sampson. Well, *real* complaints. No reason why it should be any different, working for ourselves and not him."

She, like the others, had been subjected to Mr Sampson's terrible temper on occasion. Where his nose went white at the tip, his cheeks red, and his voice took on an angry tone. He seemed to complain about twice a month, on average, about the work of each of them. Sometimes it was that a seam was too bulky – although they could not see that the seam he happened to point out was inferior to any other they had sewn. On other occasions it was a hem he charged was not straight. Though they could see no rise, or dip, or difference in width. Or a strap that was too thick. Or too thin. Or too something. They realised, now, it was his way of keeping them in line, keeping them scared he might sack them, that they would have no source of income, that the work would be taken away from them, and they would never get it back.

"I think," she went on, pausing a little and looking around the table. "I think Zussana could help me. It might be better, being women, if we approach them together. We'll have to persuade them we can work to the letter, like Mr Sampson does. And if there are two of us, if we make any mistakes and they don't take up our offer, we can repair them the next time, with the next company."

Zussana bowed her head in agreement. The others looked interested. "But how can you do it? What will you do? How can we find out the companies who give out piecework?" asked Marian Bubek in a rush.

Sylvia came in then, speaking slowly, thinking as she was talking. "He keeps a list. It's all on that clipboard. That's how I knew we were being treated unfairly by him, being paid so little when he is paid so much."

"Yes," agreed Drina. "It means that somehow we've got to get the clipboard. But without him knowing it. Or at least get a list of the businesses." She looked at the others. "But how?"

Zussana Helm spoke up again.

"We've got to separate him from the clipboard for as long as it takes to write down the names. And the addresses. And to see if there's any other useful information – like the name of the person he deals with in the company."

"Mmm." The others voiced their agreement. "What about last time?" asked Marian. "How was it that he left the clipboard in the van when you saw it, Sylvia?"

The following week, even Mr Sampson was astonished at the amount of work produced by what he thought of as his "Footscray team": "the ladies" (as he called them) working for him over in Thomas and Rendle Streets. When he turned up on Sylvia Dobroska's doorstep, she had shown him huge piles of caps and dresses and petticoats, as well as trousers and undershorts. It had taken two trips, with her carrying a load, too. Then it was on to Drina Hussein and Renda Piliavin. The same sight greeted him: pile after pile of garments, neatly stacked on the kitchen table. Load after load he transferred down to the van, Drina Hussein carrying a pile from her house, too; Renda Piliavin carrying two loads to his two.

Then it was into Rendle Street, running parallel to Thomas Street, and the clothes piled high on Marian Bubek's lounge, and stacked neatly on several chairs in Zussana Helm's kitchen. Then round the corner to Maria Trevaskis.

At each stop, eager eyes were waiting for Mr Sampson to sever himself from his clipboard; put it down in the rear of the van; deposit it on kitchen table, or chair, or lounge. Later, when he had departed, van piled high and concerned about the police stopping him because his vision was impeded by the garments which lay between the rear-vision mirror and the rear window, they compared notes.

Marian Bubek had succeeded where the others had not. Proudly she produced a list, neatly written in a firm, clear hand, of company names and suburban locations. "We can get the street names out of the telephone book," she explained. But what was really the prize were the names of Mr Sampson's contacts. The last page on the clipboard had a list of the managers or production controllers who gave him the work. And Marian had taken the whole page. "No problems," she said, as they looked at her, concerned that any minute now Mr Sampson might discover their deception, and the loss of the list. They couldn't afford to be found out at this early stage. They had hardly begun.

"There were three identical pages. A top copy and two carbons. I took one of the carbons. He probably never looks at it now, anyway. There were two other pages below it. They had the same company names, with some managers' names crossed out and new ones written in beside them. He must have just had the old list retyped, with the replacement names typed in. Seems he'll use this page for a while before he gets it retyped with any changes. And by the time he finds out the list is gone, it'll be too late."

Maria Trevaskis and Sylvia Dobroska had completed their TAFE business and accounting courses. They were confident they could run a business. They had the cash and accrual methods of accounting down to a fine art. They had paid particular attention to record creation and cash flow. They were eager to begin using their skills in the real world, rather than the artificial world of the classroom, with "pretend" businesses, and make-believe accounts.

Drina Hussein and Zussana Helm had driven, in Zussana's little mini, second-hand, battered, but with great endurance, on Mr Sampson's round. They had familiarised themselves with the route, then researched the work of the company. Sissoons Lingerie was easy: this was where Mr Sampson collected the chemise and petticoat halves, the ribbon straps, the spools of luscious lace, returning silk and satin (and acetate) garments in pink and peach and pristine white. Warners Workcaps Ltd took the caps. Drina and Zussana discovered some of the shirts and trousers also belonged to Warners.

Trudy Danielle – Ladies Lights Inc. was another lingerie company, but of the more risque kind: pinks and purples, reds and orange, and slinky black, supplemented with deep swathes of lace in contrasting colours. And the heavy-duty clothing which required thick, strong needles and strong muscles pushing the treadle up and down, up and down in a slow, regular, monotonous beat was the property of Regent Bar Overalls, Inc.

Drina and Zussana found Mr Sampson worked in with the opposition, too. Samson United Pty Ltd doled out denim and super strength cotton, almost the texture of canvas, for overalls and work trousers and shorts. Mr Sampson collected the material and delivered it around to his "ladies", picking up completed garments they had struggled with and sweated over for hours, paying the same small sum per garment, collecting the same far larger sum per garment on delivery.

Methodically, Drina Hussein and Zussana Helm worked their way through the list. At every company one or other of them managed, eventually, to follow Mr Sampson into the premises and study the layout. One or other of them observed him talking with whichever production manager was his contact, and the way he went about the job. An extra woman walking about the place was not out of the ordinary. No one noticed she was an "extra". Drina or Zussana, which ever it was, merged into the background. Even Mr Sampson didn't recognise them. On one occasion, he turned sharply, clearly having forgotten something from his car. He walked right by Zussana, showing no signs of recognition. Zussana Helm, "one of my Footscray ladies", was familiar only in Footscray, in the kitchen of her home in Rendle Street. In the corridors of Warners Workcaps Ltd, she was a stranger, never seen before and not really seen now, as he hurried outside, muttering under his breath.

Soon, Drina and Zussana were ready to report back to the others. And the others had been busy too. When Marian Bubek had purloined Mr Sampson's list of companies, she had simultaneously extracted a duplicate list of his "ladies". Marian had ridden around the streets of Footscray on her bicycle, together with Renda Piliavin, pinpointing on a map in the *Melways Directory* each home where Mr Sampson delivered materials, each home from which he collected the finished goods. Each of the outworkers was like themselves: a woman in her forties or so, with a number of children of school age, a few older, working valiantly to keep ahead. Many were single mothers. Economics made most dependent on sole parent's pension or other forms of social security. They worked to supplement a benefit or pension. Many of them spoke little or no English, as Renda and Marian found when they fell into conversation with them at the supermarket, or in the post office or greengrocer's, when they hurried to get their shopping done between Mr Sampson's visits and their work at the machines. All of them, like Maria Trevaskis, Sylvia Dobroska, Drina Hussein and the rest, could have done with more money. Each of them, like Maria and Sylvia and Drina, Marian, Renda and Zussana, should have been paid a fair wage. Unlike them, the women on Mr Sampson's list whom Marian Bubek and Renda Piliavin had located and engaged in casual conversation, were unaware of the disparity between the amounts they were paid for their work and those Mr Sampson received for it.

Around Renda's kitchen table, six of "Mr Sampson's ladies" discussed their work of the past six months. It was their final meeting. Of this phase, anyway.

Sylvia Dobroska and Maria Trevaskis outlined the plans for setting up in small business, showing the others the account books they had drawn up and the various records compiled for each of the companies who would be their customers. Each company had its own record book, name neatly printed on the cover, production manager listed on the first page, and type of stock. Each machinist had her own book, with her name on the front, and the companies whose work she was taking in listed on the first page, then appearing at intervals through the book. Each company had a section in which materials delivered could be listed on one side of the page, finished items returned on the other. There was space for listing payments for each batch of garments.

Then it was Renda and Marian Bubek's turn. They took out the map which showed the various outworkers' locations, placing it beside the list of names and addresses. There was a machinist's book, prepared by Sylvia and Maria Trevaskis, for each of the workers listed. Drina Hussein and Zussana then took out their page of company names and addresses, and production managers. These matched with the company books produced by Maria and Sylvia Dobroska.

Zussana Helm had the last report. She brought out six bottles of pills from her handbag, setting them one by one along the table top. "Prescription: Take half a tablet before retiring at night. In situations of extreme distress, take one whole tablet." Further down, at the bottom, the label ran: "Do not exceed the stated dosage without consultation with your doctor."

It had taken her six visits to the local hospital to obtain the bottles. She had told the practitioner of her galloping insomnia, her inability to sleep at all some nights, and her waking at 3.00 AM, or 4.00, or 3.30, tossing and turning, unable to return her head to the pillow and oblivion. Out had come the prescription pad. Scratching with the pen on paper, the doctor had admonished her to take half a tablet only, and then only when she found it impossible to sleep. She had returned each month, and each month the prescription pad had appeared in the first few minutes, a flourish of the pen, and the top page had been whipped out and thrust into her hand. "Next," he would shout as he opened the door and ushered her out. But now they were ready. Six lots of 200 pills was more than sufficient for two or three months. For their purpose.

They sat, six pieceworkers, satisfied with their work. Renda's kitchen had been the centre of operations for some months now. It had been transformed in the process. So had the third bedroom, vacated by Georgio. Filing cabinets lined its walls, and the bed had been replaced with a large three-drawered desk. There were shelves for the account books, the company books and the outworkers' records. The kitchen had become the boardroom, the long kitchen table and its six chairs serving them well during their meetings. With the kettle near-by, and the stove conveniently situated for hot scones when the fancy took them, they had enjoyed the past six months of planning, in between keeping up with their machining and continuing to serve Mr Sampson well. Too well.

Smiling at one another, they came back to the present. It was time to have a last look around. The basement in Renda's home had been refurbished. They walked, one after the other, down the concrete steps to the spacious room below. On the left, along the far wall, stood Georgio's old bed, clean sheets and two doonas covering the mattress. A comfortable bed. Of that, they had made sure. They didn't want too much comfort, but they were kind.

There was a record player in the corner, and a television set. The record player was an old one Sylvia Dobroska had donated. It worked, although there was a fault in the sound and it wouldn't go above the quietest notch on the volume. The television set had been Drina's. The volume had been set at a reasonable pitch, just sufficiently loud to be heard without straining the ears, not loud enough to disturb anyone nearby. The volume knob had been removed. It was securely lodged in a drawer of the desk upstairs, not far from where a tape recorder sat, stocky on the desktop, poised at just the right angle near an open pipe that went down, right down, into the basement.

Below the desk, beneath the floor, and not far from where the pipe found its outlet in the room below, a stack of records lay on a table to one side; and a comfortable old lounge chair, rescued from Marian Bubek's house, squatted at an angle near the television set. A kitchen chair, modest yet functional, stood at the end of the table. Renda pulled aside the curtain which covered, diagonally, the corner in the near righthand side of the basement. White in its newness sat the porcelain pedestal labelled "Porcelain Ware", and next to it a sparkling white sink, hot and cold taps shining in chrome. An old but serviceable washing machine stood nearby. Clean, sparse yet comfortable, each thought as she looked around.

They crowded back up the stairs, out through the stout cellar door that had been reinforced by a lock and a bolt – both on the outside, at the top of the steps, between basement and the central passageway that ran the length of Renda Piliavin's home.

"Tomorrow morning, I'll put some fruit and bread and cheese down there, and then we'll be ready," said Renda to the others. "Then – it's up to us." Solemnly, they nodded agreement.

Mr Sampson opened his eyes. His head was aching. No, it was splitting. He looked around the room, wondering where he was, what he was doing lying in a bed he did not recognise. His eyes lit upon a bowl of fruit standing on a table almost in the middle of the room. Nothing looked familiar. What had happened to him? What was the time?

He looked at his watch. In the dim light, he could see the illuminated hands. They were pointing to a quarter to three. But 2.45 PM? Or 2.45 AM? He had no idea how long he had lain, asleep, with the world spinning by.

Letting his head fall back on the pillow, he went back over the last moments he remembered. That's right! He had arrived home to find a note from his wife, telling him she had left him. That she couldn't stand it any more. That now the children were grown, there was no reason for their living together. That she had seen a solicitor several months ago, and that papers would soon arrive for settlement of property and for the divorce. She had told the solicitor she and Mr Sampson had not been sharing a bedroom for years, and that she had given up cooking and cleaning for him a long time ago. That he had had to do his own laundry, or send it out. That she had shopped for herself alone. That she and he had nothing in common, and even the children talked to them as if they were separate beings, now. Coleman and Rangoon, Solicitors, had told her she would likely qualify for a divorce in the circumstances. That she and Mr Sampson would be considered, legally, to have been "living separately and apart" for more than twelve months, and that this was all the law required, now, for a divorce to become final. She was divorcing him. And she was never coming back.

Mr Sampson sighed, putting his hand to his forehead. Well, that was that. She was gone. Now he only had to make sure she didn't get any of the property he thought of as his. The house. The car. The television set. The shares in BHP he had kept from her. The block of land down at Aireys Inlet. The flats out at Croydon. The houses at Coburg and Preston. His mind automatically began adding up what he was worth – then he was drawn back rudely to the present. Where was he? Certainly not at home in Hawthorn, the four bedroomed home he had sweated and striven for, day in, day out, paying out too much to the outworkers. Getting back too little from the companies. Building up the business through his own muscle and brains. She had played no part.

Four children, yes. But she wanted them. And she had to look after them. Wasn't any great difficulty, anyway. Not that he could see. Every night, when he came back from having a quick drink with his colleagues at the club, after a long hard day on the road, driving round and around, up and down, between the houses, collecting and delivering, pushing those women to work harder, lazy buggers...Every night, the children were in bed. Not a peep out of them. Good as gold. No problems. No trouble at all for Meg, he was sure...She had always had a meal waiting for him, in those early times, until the last few years when the children left home. No trouble at all. Babies turned into children, went to school, came home, did their homework. Grew up without him having to lift a finger. Well, a few belts now and then, but nothing serious. And Meg. Meg! Well, that was all she did all day – sitting around, little bit of housework here, flap with a duster once in a while. House always spic and span – but because it was built that way. All mod cons. He had bought her everything, that woman, and now she had walked out on him. It was too much.

But – but where was he? Nowhere he knew, that's for sure. He raised his head from the pillow again, then lifted the doonas and thought to test out his legs. Slowly, slowly, he lifted one. It felt like lead. It flopped back on to the mattress. He tried again. This time, he got his right leg out of the bed and on to the floor. The warm carpet came up to hit the bottom of his right foot. Then he began with his left leg. Slowly, slowly again he managed to make it follow the right. Then he began to lift his torso into a sitting position. At first, his body flopped back, refusing to obey the simplest instructions. Then, at last, he was upright.

Leaning his back against the wall, he surveyed the room from a new vantage point. No windows! That was the first thing that registered with him. No windows!

Was he in prison? But how could that be?

He thought more rapidly, now. Sitting up had somehow given his brain a jolt, bringing it into the more recent past.

He recalled driving out of the house that morning – well, the morning he found the note from Meg, saying she was leaving. Who knew what morning it was. He had lost all sense of time.

Out he had driven, on his usual rounds. Picked up material from Sissoons, and Regent Bar Overalls, and the others. Made his way to Footscray and the outworkers. He had visited Dobroska, and Hussein, and... It was coming back to him. He had arrived at Piliavin with a terrible head. Meg's leaving him had at last begun hitting home. If she wanted to up and leave, let her. But what would happen to the property? He had heard all about the Family Court and the *Family Law Act* from Jack Denoot, one of his friends at the club. "Take you for all you've got, nowadays," he had said in a conversation where the men sat round talking about what was wrong with the world. The way the women were taking over. "Take you to the cleaners, mate. I tell you," said Jack, "It's all one way, now. A man hasn't got a chance. Hasn't got a bloody chance." He wasn't sure that Jack was right, but he didn't want to lose *anything*.

Just as he came into the Piliavin kitchen to collect the piles of overalls and caps and nightgowns, he had smelt the blissful aroma of hot, sugary pastry. Hot pastry topped with creamy icing and currants! Or hot pastry and honey and raisins! Years since he'd had any. That Meg. Gave up on cooking for him. Sentenced him to takeaways. McDonald's. Colonel Sanders. Red Rooster. Pizza Hut. Ahh! How his stomach longed for a good, wholesome, decent, homemade pastry. Just this once. Just this once he wanted to sit down in a homely kitchen, taking him back to the days of his childhood and youth, when women were mothers and wives, and didn't have any jumped up ideas in their heads...

He had sat at the table. One of his Footscray ladies – Mrs Piliavin, he was sure, as he thought back – had served him up sugared pastry and raspberry jam, with something creamy and sweet dribbling down the sides. And tea. Good, strong, home brewed. The way he liked it. Funny, the way these foreigners picked up things so quickly. The old fashioned way. Old fashioned, but streets ahead of this new fangled stuff. Tea bags. Not real tea. He sipped the brew. He ate the pastries. There were a lot of them. He rested his head on his hand. He remembered nothing more.

Now – here he was. And again, *where?*

If Mr Sampson had but known it, above him, whizzing away on her new electric sewing machine, sat Renda Piliavin. She had begun on the overalls today, sewing the seams and the crutch, the bands and the braces, with a will. Outworkers Aboard had been in full swing for three days. Zussana Helm and Drina Hussein had had no trouble working to Mr Sampson's schedule with the companies, picking up the materials on time, delivering them along his route. The production managers had simply accepted their explanation. That Mr Sampson was down the coast for a few weeks, supervising some building, and he had hired them to take deliveries and return the finished goods. Old Sampson (as he had become known) was getting on, anyway. Time to get the younger ones in. Sissoons, and Warners Workcaps, and Trudy Danielle – Ladies Lights, and the others, didn't care, so long as the work was done, on time, and well. Sampson had always performed. No reason to suspect anyone he hired couldn't collect and deliver, and ensure the goods were in the right shape. Even if they were women. Drina and Zussana collected and delivered, on time. By the third day, production managers around Footscray, Richmond and environs had forgotten Mr Sampson ever existed.

Zussana and Drina had made the rounds of the outworkers, too. Delivering and collecting. And paying for work done.

At each home, they introduced themselves to the woman who had for so long worked to Mr Sampson's heavy requirements. And light payments. They told her of the new business approach that was to be taken by them, in Mr Sampson's absence. Gave each of them an account book, to record the material in, the garments out. With a fat column on the righthand side for recording payments.

It was then that they received the first glances of shock. Even horror. Or fear. Though quickly passing, with Drina and Zussana's assurances.

What was happening, wondered the workers. Perhaps they weren't hearing correctly. Paesi Dolma queried the amounts twice. Fatima Abdulla pressed her hand to the curve of her right ear as she timidly asked Drina to repeat the amounts she had quoted for working caps and overalls. Ten dollars? Twenty dollars? That couldn't be right!

It was right. Bemused, bewildered, but buoyed by the prospect, Fatima Abdulla dutifully recorded the amounts in her book, next to the items she had completed, and the quantities. Paesi Dolma solemnly wrote in the figures, guided by Zussana Helm's clear voice. "A fair day's work for a fair day's pay," Zussana had said to her, as she had said to the others, when they questioningly gazed at the wad of notes Drina had placed in their hands. "That's the motto of Outworkers Aboard," added Drina, as she and Zussana walked down the steps, making their way back to the van and on to the next address.

When he woke again, Mr Sampson saw a short flight of steps leading up, out of the room. Staggering from the bed, he felt his way along the wall and crawled up them. He banged his fist on the door. It was solid. He tried to shake it. It stood firm. Hanging his head, he returned the way he had come, and sat down on the kitchen chair that stood beside the table. Picking up a banana, he peeled it, sinking his teeth into the ripe flesh with gratitude. Then a low, disembodied voice broke into his thoughts. "Mr Sampson," it said. He looked up, darting a swift glance to the steps. Was he to be liberated soon?

There was no one there. The door showed only its thick panels, sturdy and immoveable, between him and the outside. The voice, paying no attention to his agitation, went inexorably on.

"For years you have sweated us outworkers and many others. We do not accept you have any right to do this. Your treatment of women workers has been unlawful and immoral. Australia has award wages and rates of pay. Outworkers are entitled to a living wage."

The disembodied voice was floating about in the atmosphere, somewhere in the vicinity of the ceiling. Where was it coming from? Mr Sampson got up from the table, his legs pressing against the hard edge of the chair, his eyes looking up, his head raised, straining to see. The voice would not stop.

"We recognise you have no concept of fair play and fair wages. We have therefore decided to reassess your business, and to adjust rates of pay for all workers on your payroll. From now on, workers will receive fair payments for work done."

Fair payments, he thought to himself. I'll give them "fair payments". I'm the one who determines what's fair and what isn't.

The voice ignored his reddening face, and went on:

"You will remain here, well looked after, fed and with basic conveniences, until you recognise the error of your ways. You will be allowed to go free only when you sign the documents you see on the table in front of you."

There was a brief pause. Then: "Outworkers Aboard has spoken." The voice stopped.

Mr Sampson looked down, scarcely recovered from the hollow intonation of the messenger, and saw a neatly typed document set out before him on the shiny veneer table top, one white corner under the fruit bowl to secure it in place.

The document had a "with compliments" slip attached to it by a paperclip. The slip read: "Outworkers Aboard". Underneath it, the document read like a contract. It was a contract. In fact, it was a transfer of business agreement. It said he agreed to hand over to Outworkers Aboard his van, his lists of outworkers, his lists of company suppliers and customers, for the sum of $1.00. One dollar! And there was a requirement that he sign every cheque in the cheque book which he now saw had been placed alongside the fruit bowl and the note. Grabbing it up, he saw, yes, it was his cheque book. For the secret account he kept — well, one of the accounts he hoped his wife didn't know about. It currently held $150,000 on an interest bearing deposit, which he had arranged to be paid direct into the cheque account on maturity, while he decided what to do with it. He had been thinking about putting it down as a deposit on a block of flats in Heidelberg. But... now...

Opening the cheque book, his astounded eyes saw the words "Outworkers Aboard" printed neatly on the "Pay" line. What a nerve! He flipped through the book. There were six blank cheques left. Every one was made out to Outworkers Aboard. He looked back at the document of transfer. If he signed it, and the cheques, he would be signing away the $150,000, and his business. His livelihood. His fortune. *His* money.

Outworkers Aboard wanted him to sign one cheque to the amount of $10,000, one for $40,000, and one for $100,000. Those were the figures printed in, in even, business-like figures. And he was to sign the remaining blanks. Just in case there was any interest, he supposed. And why? They were mad. Some mumbo jumbo about recompense for the payments he had failed to make to the pieceworkers all the years they had worked for him — at a pittance. "Pittance" was the word used in the document. It was not his word. Paid them properly. And well. Couldn't have made any money, silly women, if he hadn't arranged everything for them. Cultivated the contacts. Got the contracts. Picked up the materials. Delivered here, there and everywhere. Showed them how to do a good job... Well, even Mr Sampson was honest with himself, sometimes. Got one of the experienced workers to show the new ones what to do. But he had kept them up to the mark. Made sure they had known what standards were required. Given them a blast once every two weeks or so, just to make sure they didn't slip. Why, heavens, they'd have been lost without him. Him exploiting them? It was the other way around.

He grew quite indignant, sitting there, and almost screwed note and contract into an untidy ball. In anger and defiance he almost tore the cheque book in half, the blank cheques into tiny pieces. But prudence stopped him. He never knew. Maybe – maybe what they wrote... Outworkers Aboard wrote... was true. They wouldn't let him out until he signed. He sat, staring into the distance, his eyes meeting the white wall opposite, but seeing nothing.

Two months later, Outworkers Aboard was expanding rapidly. But not so rapidly as to draw unwelcome attention. Maria Trevaskis and Sylvia Dobroska worked on the books full-time. They had taken over Renda's third bedroom, painting it and putting up bookshelves, and bringing in another desk.

The lists of pieceworkers grew. The lists of companies took up several pages. Mr Sampson's old clipboard hung on the wall, a trophy, unused. There were two telephones on the desk in the second bedroom – renamed the main office. And one on the desk in the "annex". They were contemplating investing in a Commander telephone, with twelve lines. They didn't need twelve lines yet, "But you never know", said Maria, as her fingers flew over the face of the calculator before her on the desk.

Sylvia, sitting across from Maria, glanced down at the tape recorder to one side, checking that it was working. Yes. The automatic switch flipped on, and the tape began to run. She looked up, then, her expression one of concentration. "Y-e-s," she said, slowly. "Be prepared. No good expanding and not having the infra-structure to support it, as they said at the TAFE. You're right, Maria. Better take it back to the next meeting."

In the basement, Mr Sampson sat, eating his dinner. He knew it was dinner, because he was sitting in front of the television set, looking at the screen where the 6.00 PM newscast was flashing and shining, earnest male and female faces peering out at him in swift succession. But never a report on *his* disappearance. No one missed him. Even his children must have forgotten he ever existed. He hadn't seen them much, anyway, he thought.

Slowly, he cut the large chop that lay on the plate, smothered in some sort of homemade sauce. His eyes glazing as he tasted the sauce and meat, trance like he directed knife and fork back toward the meal, piling white, thick, whipped potato on to his fork, and pressing succulent, round, green peas into the mash.

Not for a long time – since his childhood, he thought, sentimentally – had he eaten so well. Not for years had he tasted meat so tender, so tasty; vegetables so fresh, so crisp, so tempting. Not since he could remember, had he been presented with bread and butter custard. And he was learning to like "that foreign muck" as he had called it, too. Meat wrapped in vine leaves. Chicken and fish cooked in the most extraordinary ways. Odd looking sausage, which tasted rather good. Lamb, cooked in a strange but tempting way. Sweet, homemade halva. Italian bread sticks. Even heavy black bread he was developing a taste for. He sat back, rubbing his stomach without thinking. He was developing quite a pot.

Then "the voice" started up again, interrupting his meal and the noises coming from the screen. Or, at least, it was one of the voices. He caught the different accents, slightly different intonations. But the message was always the same. He had listened to the voices and the words often enough. Now, he knew the message by heart: "Mr Sampson." Pause. Recommence.

"For years you have sweated us outworkers and many others. We do not accept you have any right to do this. Your treatment of women workers has been unlawful and immoral..."

On and on it went, with the same message. Over and over, for the first week, it had run every six hours, starting at 12 noon, then repeated (with a different voice) at 6.00 PM, then at midnight (with yet another voice). He had been woken by it, the first time he heard it in the middle of the night, the cellar black, the voice coming out of nowhere, echoing around the room. He had almost been driven mad by it. But Mr Sampson vowed he would not give in.

The next week, it had come every hour, on the hour. That went on until he thought he could bear it no more. But the following week, the times had varied again. It had come on at any time, so he was unable to calculate when it would next sound out. There was no pattern to it. There might be a pause of four hours, then it was on again in half an hour. Then no more voices until eight hours later. He didn't know if this was worse, not knowing when the message would come out of the darkness or into the flickering light of the television, or being programmed with a regularity that made him tense his muscles (or whatever he felt was left of them) when "the time" came.

Sighing, he looked again at the transfer of business document. Maybe it wasn't so mad. Maybe... maybe...

Mr Sampson sat in his cellar, his chin on his hand, listening to a melancholy recording of "O Sole Mio". Slowly, he peeled a banana. Almost without noticing he was eating it, he thrust the end of the fruit into his mouth. His jaws chomping methodically, he looked at the white wall ahead. Rising, he walked, almost trance-like, over to the television set. He flicked the switch. The screen began to shimmer.

Then, the voice broke in: "From now on, workers will receive fair payments for work done." Pause. "You will remain here..."

"You will remain here. You will remain here." The words reverberated in his head.

Ten weeks on, Mr Sampson signed. He had, surprisingly, rather enjoyed his period in isolation. (Apart from the message. The voices. The infernal voices.) No complaints about the bed. Firm mattress. Soft coverings. No problems with the entertainment. (When no voice sounded, like a clear reverberation in a drain pipe.) Television. Records. No difficulties with washing. Clean clothes, too.

He had realised, early on, that Outworkers Aboard must be drugging some of his food, or his drinks. But he couldn't stop eating. Or drinking. Every night, he slept soundly – except when, bleary eyed, he woke momentarily to the voice coming out of the darkness, with the message. And when he finally woke, properly, in the mornings, he knew someone had been there, making sure he had washing powder for the washing machine, leaving fresh bread for his breakfast, which he put in the toaster, leaving hot sausages and eggs, or strange, foreign looking food that tasted good.

He had rebelled against using the washing powder, at least for the first week. But he had succumbed, in the end, to washing sheets and shirt, trousers and underwear. He couldn't sit about in the same clothes day in, day out. Week in, week out, as it had become.

Monday night, the night he picked up the pen and wrote his signature on the bottom of the document, and signed each blank cheque in the book, making them out in the amounts dictated to him, he went to bed resigned to the morning. And in the morning? Although he had been treated well, his head screamed – it wasn't right. It JUST WAS NOT RIGHT.

He had been cooped up for weeks, in a basement somewhere in Footscray. *Forced* to listen to voices telling him the same message, over and over. Business down the drain. Taken over. And what of Meg. Probably she'd moved back into Hawthorn. Maybe settled herself in so well that he would not be able to get back in, himself. And her solicitors had probably traced everything he had kept from her, by now. Searched and documented everything. Knew what he was worth to the penny. He'd had no chance to cover his tracks.

But...would Outworkers Aboard let him go?

Late in the afternoon, long after they had picked up the signed documents and cashed the cheques, they stood before him in a line: Maria Trevaskis, Drina Hussein, Renda Piliavin, Zussana Helm, Marian Bubek and Sylvia Dobroska. "We are Outworkers Aboard, Mr Sampson. We pay the pieceworkers fair rates, proper pay, with decent conditions," they said. The voices rang in his ears, the tones oh, so familiar.

"We've put the money into a trust fund, for the workers, Mr Sampson," added Maria Trevaskis. "It belongs to them. And to us. We all worked hard, long hours for little pay. You exploited us, Mr Sampson."

"It'll be used for insurance and superannuation, and for any emergencies," put in Sylvia Dobroska. "Just a standby. But what the workers need and deserve."

There was a short silence. "You...You...You...WOMEN!" shouted Mr Sampson. "You...You..."

"No point in carrying on like that, Mr Sampson. No one can hear you," said Renda Piliavin. "Do you want to leave, or do you want to stay here longer?"

"Probably best to go quietly, Mr Sampson, don't you agree," added Marian Bubek.

"I won't go quietly. You'll pay for this. You'll pay. It's my business," stormed Mr Sampson. "I'll get it back...I'll have you prosecuted. You'll spend years – *years* in prison. You wait."

"No, you wait, Mr Sampson," said Zussana Helm, in her quiet, but firm, voice. "No point in telling anyone about this, is there?"

Drina Hussein moved slightly forward, her expression calm, her stance resolute.

"Your former customers have forgotten all about you, Mr Sampson. The women you called *your* workers don't remember a thing about you, except the low rates you paid them. We'll have any signs of you in this basement cleared out in less than an hour. Every fingerprint, every trace gone. We're hard workers, Mr Sampson. You know that."

"And," broke in Renda. "Takes nothing to wipe a tape, Mr Sampson. Done in a trice." Sylvia Dobroska nodded.

"No point in carrying on, really, is there, Mr Sampson. You won't go to the police. They won't believe you. They'll laugh at you. *Your* pieceworkers winning out. *Your* pieceworkers taking over. *Your* pieceworkers paying themselves decent wages, making the business boom by treating women workers with respect.

"Report to the police? Tell the *Herald Sun*? The *Age*? Think of the talkback programmes. And television, Mr Sampson. 'Present Times.' 'Cover Story.' 'Two Hemispheres'…'Finch on the Box.' Make wonderful television…"

When he left the basement, Mr Sampson was not a reformed man. Nor was he a reformed businessman. But he was a quieter man, a somewhat chastened man. And he left behind him a revolution in piecework.

Mobile Meals

MR PARSONS WAS kicking up a stink as usual. Dorreen and Josie could hear his voice as they came down the driveway in the van. As they got out, taking a canister with them in each hand, the noise grew louder, until it reached a crescendo as they reached the Parsons' frontdoor.

"Don't come in interrupting me when I'm watching the cricket," shouted the voice. "When's a man to get a bit of peace and quiet nowadays?" they heard, shortly followed by: "Out, out, out, woman. The television's mine."

As they stood on the steps, Dorreen with her hand poised above the buzzer, they could almost see the scene inside: Mr Parsons pushing and shoving at his wife, blustering and booming, pressing her out of the television room and into the cold hallway. Then they saw him, clear as a picture before their eyes, retiring back into the comfortable lounge chair in front of the television set, putting his feet up on the footrest after adjusting the electric heater blazing away to one side, and taking up the glass of beer that he invariably kept within reach. They looked at one another. Was this the last straw for Mr Parsons? Their eyes met. Imperceptibly, they nodded. Then, Dorreen pressed the bell. Mrs Parsons opened the frontdoor, her eyes suspiciously red.

Dorreen Simmons and Josie Smart had worked together for years. They began doing volunteer work at the Jones Family. On reflection, thought Dorreen, her mind idly running back over the past one day, when it was very hot and she sat, comfortably cool on the verandah in the shade of the big old gum tree growing in the back garden: "That was how we met."

Josie had been inspecting and sorting clothes donated to the Jones Family. In one pile she placed those ready to go to the drycleaners. In another she put those which were beyond redemption, to be consigned to the scrap basket for quilting or mending more worthy garments. In a third pile went those which would see their last days out as cleaning rags or dusters. She put to one side the ones requiring further work: buttons to be replaced, sagging hems to be stitched, tears to be mended, lace to be repaired.

Dorreen and Josie had been introduced, and for the next five years or so they worked alongside one another, regularly sorting and piling, then bundling, packaging and tying, Jones Family donations.

Then, Dorreen had moved from one side of the harbour to the other and, for her, travelling time became wearisome. She and Josie looked around for something else. They were still into good works, and wanted it to remain so. But what was closer to home? For some nine or ten months they joined the workers at St Mary de Magdalene. But some of the interest had gone out of the secondhand clothes' trade. It seemed that, lately, people were holding on to their "good" garments, wearing them just one more season. The clothes coming in were more often of poor quality, with drooping peplums, ragged stitching, grubbinesses that could not be removed, even with firstclass dry cleaning or laundering. "Perhaps it's the economic downturn," said Josie to Dorreen.

"No wonder the ragtrade's on a downer. Everyone's seeing the new season in with the old or recycled. Buying new accessories, perhaps, but no new dresses. No new anything."

Then they worked as a duo for another few years, looking after disgruntled youth. Each became an Honourary Probation Officer, an official title given them by the government, through the recommendation of the Probation and Parole Branch of the Welfare Department. Together they organised community work for juvenile delinquents...Well, that term had gone out of favour. It had an old fashioned flavour to it, although Dorreen and Josie were fond of it, and used it often. They had been young adults in the 1950s and '60s, when bodgies and widgies

had flooded the scene, and the escapades of juvenile delinquents filled the pages of the tabloid press. Today, it was
"young offenders". And it was young offenders for whom they
arranged work. They combed the countryside for pensioners
(well, "mature citizens") in need of their lawns mowed, weeds
pulled, sweeping up of the leaves from paths, a bit of painting
about the place: the front fence, the pickets at the back, the
garden shed; nothing too complicated, that youth could muck
up, but nothing so simple and easy that it took no application,
no concentration, no industry.

Dorreen and Josie consulted with various elderly citizens'
organisations; community bodies; local councils. They came up
with all sorts of tasks to which young people, gone slightly
wrong, could apply themselves. And which, it was hoped,
would get "youth" back on the proverbial straight and narrow.
But, eventually, that job came to an end. The government
decided there was no more room for "Honouraries". The profes-
sionals took over. Josie and Dorreen were "out".

It was Dorreen who thought of Mobile Meals. It came to her,
when she and Josie were scouring the countryside for community work for their youthful probationers, that there were too
many old people out there needing a helping hand. "When
you're old, Josie," Dorreen said, leaning back on a chair in the
kitchen of the flat she and Josie now shared (they had moved in
together when Josie's husband died of a heart attack at 53; he'd
had a good life and it simply came to an end, just like that),
"when you're old," she repeated, nodding sagely, "You can't be
bothered to cook properly as you do when you're young and
hungry. They just let themselves go. Don't realise they've got
to eat, whether they're having hunger pangs or not. They tend
to forget."

She nodded again at Josie who was standing at the stove,
stirring a pot of soup for the evening meal.

"It's a bit the reverse of the suicide syndrome...You know.
The one who takes a couple of sleeping pills, then wakes up and
forgets she's done it, and takes some more. And before you
know where you are, its ambulances, and flashing lights, and
she's for the emergency ward and the stomach pump. Well, with

31

the oldies, they think they've actually had dinner, when they haven't. Then they think they've had supper, when not a thing, not one thing – not a crust, not an apricot, not even a sausage – has passed their lips. They wake up in the morning thinking they've eaten breakfast. And they sail through the day thinking at every step they've just lunched or dined or morning-tead, or whatever. Then they pass out from exhaustion, fatigue, starvation. And for them its the flashing lights and casualty. And instead of stomach pumps taking it all out, it's stomach pumps putting it all in."

She paused. "It's time all that was ended. Smartly. And it's Mobile Meals for us, Josie."

Josie looked at her. "Mmmm. Have heard of it, now I come to think of it. Don't they – don't they do the cooking for them. Do it in their own kitchens or something, then take it out on rounds, deliver the lunches and dinners and breakfasts, so that no one does starve. Everyone eats well...Depending on the cooking, of course. But if you're doing the cooking, you have to be good. Anyway, good wholesome food. I guess that's all they want?"

"All they want?" roared Dorreen. "That's *pre*cisely what they want. Just what's good for you and me and everyone. Good, wholesome, home-made cooking. And that's what we do around here, anyway." She looked at Josie, still standing at the stove, stirring the pot. Josie looked back.

They had joined up soon after, putting their names down with Lady Sanderson as volunteers with Mobile Meals. Lady Sanderson, she of the stretched face, as Dorreen called it pointing out to Josie the way the skin smoothed paper-thin over the cheek bones, and hugged the edges of her ears and upper reaches of her forehead, folds nipped and tucked, joins hidden, mostly, under the fringes of hair that coiled over her face. Neatly, mind you. But artfully coiled, nonetheless.

Lady Sanderson ran the roster, with grim efficiency. She knew talent when she saw it, and as soon as she saw Josie and Dorreen, she knew she was on to it. The duo exuded competence. It ran out of their pores. It shone from their powderless faces. It glowed from their eyes. It transmitted itself in energy from their workaday limbs. Their positive exuberance was ever present. To Lady Sanderson, it was palpable. Just the right level of enthusiasm, just the right degree of well-wishing. Not dreary, so unpleasant for the recipients of the largesse of Mobile Meals. Yet not intrusive, so that the elderly were overcome with a too powerful sense of jollity which, in one's later years, Lady Sanderson had noticed, translated in the older mind into loudness. Noise. "Be calm. Be calm," she had had to say to several women who had come in offering their services. They had been smartly moved on, in the end. Couldn't have the clientele being upset, whether they were paying customers, or charity cases. The elderly deserved respect, Lady Sanderson often told herself. And they needed simple joy, not noisy raging, she declared privately. And Lady Sanderson's thoughts were always, but always, translated into public action.

She knew at once that Josie and Dorreen would not have to be "moved on". She knew at once that, despite Dorreen's slightly unkempt appearance on occasion, and whatever Josie's rotundity of figure, the duo were "just right" for Mobile Meals. She telephoned them two days later, not wanting to seem too anxious to get them on board, yet not wishing to run the risk of losing them to some other good cause. And it was necessary to snap up the good workers almost on the spot, particularly now. Right now. There was WAR in the charity world at present. All began with a falling out between the ladies (she snorted to herself) of the Purple, Green and White brigade, and the "jumped ups" (or that's how the P, G and W's described them) of the "Muzette Bubbles Auxiliary". With a name like that, who could blame them? And "auxiliary" to what? was the question.

But Lady Sanderson put it all to one side. Who cared what P, G and W's and the MBA's were doing. There was work to be done. Real work. Not all this "society" flibberty-gibberting. And as far as she was concerned, it *was* being done by Mobile Meals. Down to earth, necessary, essential, the basics. That's where she directed her energies. And she was glad to add the energies of Dorreen and Josie to the task. Lady Sanderson heaved sighs of relief. Not so easy, nowadays, to get the ones who would really do the work.

Lady Sanderson's judgement was well rewarded. Off went Josie and Dorreen with a will. Once a week, they worked in the kitchen, a large, welcoming room at Mobile Meal headquarters in George Street. Josie had been particularly skilled at introducing new menus and meals on to the list. She was adept at ferreting out, or devising, recipes which could be easily made; did not lose their taste or "specialness" through being cooked in bulk; could be transported far and wide without losing their freshness and "just cooked" flavour and appearance. She was a marvel, thought Lady Sanderson at regular intervals. A real marvel.

For the other four days (and sometimes five, when Mobile Meals was pressed, and Lady Sanderson called to implore them to help out, and they came, always, without demur, without complaint, ever cheerful, ever ready, ever "right for the road") Josie and Dorreen drove around in one of the many delivery vans. Well, they weren't vans, really. A fleet of smart red Minis, zipping about the roads, beetling about the lanes. Following the well-worn route of happy Mobile Meals' customers – well, clients, really. And the numbers kept increasing. With elderly people it was inevitable that they would all go off the list at some time. But Mobile Meals kept the numbers up. When one customer – client – passed on, peacefully leaving the world and the daily delights of Mobile Meals' offerings, there was always another to be added.

Dorreen was particularly adept at locating new couples, or singles, for adding to the list. Dorreen and Josie's route was constantly being added to, the "drop offs" (as they called them in the trade: had to find a name to cover the inevitable depletion of the ranks) being replaced smartly, with more couples, more singles. And it was rare that both sides of a couple removed themselves simultaneously from the lists held by Mobile Meals. No, usually it was the case that Mr Jones, or Mr Smith, or Mr Brown or Mr White, "went" before Mrs Smith, and Mrs Brown, Mrs Jones, and Mrs White. Lady Sanderson often reflected on this. She had suffered in the same way. Sir Reg (not for him the snobbishness of reverting to "Reginald" just because he had gained a knighthood) had gone years ago. Quite peacefully. But gone, nonetheless.

She had woken one morning and glanced over at his bed, as she had so often before. And his body had been very still. Well, it usually was, early in the morning. But her observant eye had noticed there was not even the gentle rise and fall of the counterpane, or the soft brrrpng noise his nostrils usually emitted in sleep. And she had thought – yes, privately she had to be honest with herself – slightly, ever so slightly, joyfully, "Maybe he's gone."

And he had "gone". She called in Dr Fraser, the family doctor. Very nice man, a gentleman. Respectable, caring, concerned. Even he, gentle old pixie, thought she would be devastated. They had just celebrated their fifty year anniversary. Fifty years is a long time.

A very long time, she had thought, privately.

The funeral was beautiful. Lots of lovely white chrysanthemums and red roses, and wreaths of golden daffodils entwined with deep, sea-green ivy. All sent to the local hospital. Never, but never, buried with Sir Reg, or left to droop and die at the graveside. His wish, it was. And there wasn't a graveside as such, anyway. Sir Reg was a firm believer in cremation. Everything in its place, and a clean end to every-thing. Ashes to ashes, he was wont to intone, particularly in his later years. Anticipating, no doubt.

Lady Sanderson drew herself back to the present with a start. One of the problems of growing old, she had noticed, was the tendency to drift off into reveries, remembrances of things past. Where was she? Oh yes, reflecting on the good work of Josie and Dorreen. The regular disappearance of names from the lists, and the regular recruitment of new names. The men went first, but the wives lived on, and on. They seemed to get a new lease of life. Just as she had, with Reg gone. Why, she had flung herself into Mobile Meals with a vengeance. Altered it, in eight short years, from being the poor country cousin of the charities, to the thriving metropolitan nexus of services to the

elderly that it was. They had expanded from the eastern suburbs and the north shore, out into the west. And Dorreen had
come to her just a few days ago, talking of expansion into the
country. Lady Sanderson's eyes shone. More work to be done.
This was living. She thanked god (and Reg) for the long years
of sheer happiness she saw stretching before her.

Dorreen and Josie were collecting up the Wednesday dinners.
They were scheduled to run their usual route, the route that
included Mr and Mrs Parsons. Or Mrs and Mr Parsons, as Lady
Sanderson always titled "her" married couples.

Despite the stretched skin, she had a brain, that woman,
Dorreen often thought to herself, confiding in Josie her ad-
miration for Lady Sanderson's get up and go, her existence in
the real world of the living, her recognition of the important
things in life, her acknowledgement of the right and proper
order of things.

Josie had been particularly careful to make sure the meal was
something Mr Parsons really liked. Rarely did he utter an
appreciative word, that was true. But they knew, by the sound
of his slurping lips, invariably following them out of the door
after their regular delivery to him and Mrs Parsons, that he ate
everything. And that some meals were his favourites. Roast
pork and a good, rich gravy. Followed by crisp apple tart,
swimming with large, luscious sultanas in fresh clotted cream.
If it were to be his last meal, then it should be a good one. It
would be.

Josie and Dorreen set out, good-humoured determination on
their faces. The delivery round went well. And when they
reached the Parsons' household, they knew they had made no
error. Loud voices reached them as they drew into the driveway,
the noise increasing as they strode up the stairs and toward the
frontdoor.

Well, it was not really loud *voices,* Josie corrected herself. It
was a loud voice. And a much softer one, timidly responding to
whatever it was he was on about this time. What was it? They
didn't have to strain their ears to know that it was about the

television set yet again. And about Mr Parsons' inalienable right to it. And his inalienable right to occupation of the television room, when he chose; and to the electric heater; and to his beer – brought to him by Mrs Parsons, treading so softly, trying so hard not to antagonise.

"As if treading softly would assist her to escape his wrath and his rage," Josie had often said, knowingly, to Dorreen.

Dorreen lifted her hand and pressed the buzzer. The door opened. There was a brief, though welcoming smile, the smile of a woman bowed down. It was a smile Josie and Dorreen had met so often, on their journeys with Mobile Meals. It was a smile that had, on other front stoops, in other houses, in other streets, called for the same response.

The canisters disappeared into the house, the larger ones for Mr Parsons. The smaller, as ever, for Mrs Parsons. Never a chance, not in this household, as elsewhere, that Mrs Parsons would eat Mr Parsons' share. Never a chance she would take the large for herself, not the small. Not a skerrick of a danger that Mr Parsons' last meal would reach the wrong lips, the wrong mouth, the wrong stomach. Or that the "special ad-ditives", so finely crushed and mixed by Josie into the creamy gravy in the large cannister, not the small; and sprinkled on the sultana rich apples in their fine castor-sugared pastry, in the large cannister, not the small, would reach the wrong oesophagus, the wrong capillaries, the wrong bloodstream.

"Eat well, Mrs Parsons," intoned Josie, gently. "Eat well, Mr Parsons," Dorreen whispered firmly. Lightly, jauntily, even, they returned to the Mini, the meals, their list and the remainder of the day.

Mobile Meals' breakfasts were a joy to behold, Lady Sanderson thought daily. What other meal delivery service could produce steaming hot muffins, crisp sizzling bacon, warm brown toast. Not for Mobile Meals the soggy and the lukewarm.

She gazed out of the rear window of Mobile Meals' headquarters. There they were, bright and early as always, Josie and Dorreen loading the van. Out they whizzed, disappearing into the morning traffic. "What's doing today?" She wondered. "Any newies to be added to our lists? Any additional houses to be noted, any new couples? Any new singles? Any old singles for that matter...a couple rendered single by a sad passing on..."

She reflected on the utility and care combined in Mobile Meals. Serving meals was prime work. But it was not just serving meals. So often, she recalled, when the man of the house passed on, Mobile Meals was first on the scene. Josie and Dorreen had proved themselves so proficient at that, too. Always there, at the ready, when the woman of the house discovered the passing. Ever there, with care and concern, to assist her in calling the doctor. Ever ready with cups of strong tea and a crisp, though discreet, biscuit or two. Not only (although very importantly) for the bereaved wife – the widow. Cups of tea and the discreet, crisp biscuit – or two, or three – for the doctor, too. Just to bear him up while he made his final diagnosis, wrote his last certificate. Never any great brain power needed to determine the cause for the passing on of elderly gentlemen. Old age. Heart attack. Died in his sleep. Whatever. She knew well with Sir Reg that that was how it worked. Call the doctor. Doctor comes. Tests the pulse. Stethoscope over the heart. And that was basically it.

Sometimes they caused a lot trouble in life, husbands, she remarked to herself, just as Josie and Dorreen were remarking, without speaking, to one another as they stood in the kitchen of the Parsons' (singular) household. But no trouble at all in death.

Creative Accounting

SHE WHIZZED THROUGH the housework. It was her turn to collect the children from childcare today, and she didn't want to be late. That would never do. "Wouldn't it just bring down the wrath of the others," she thought, smiling to herself, but concerned as well. To be late at such a crucial time would be extraordinary, certainly. All the afternoons she had taken her turn in picking up the kiddies, and particularly on afternoons like this one, it had never happened. And she didn't mean there to be a first time.

To the outside observer, Suzanne Renfree was a "housewife" just like any other of the thousands of young women, wives and mothers, working away all over the world, caring for husband, home and children. In her case, it was one child, just as it was for Janie Rowe and Megan Downes, her "girlfriends", as her husband Nick called them. Kate was three-and-a-half, enjoying her time at childcare, where Ms Costain came up with all sorts of ideas, using discarded egg packets, the centre cardboard from used toilet rolls, plasticine, fancy buttons. You name it, and she would use it. And the children delighted in the fun of being "grownup". Of going off each morning, just like Daddy, taking a kindie case with peanut butter sandwich, an apple or banana. Sometimes a mandarin. As Daddy did.

Janie's Sam went to the same childcare centre, in Russell Street in the city. He too loved the days spent being "independent", with Ms Costain, in the old but comfortable building. He and Kate got on well together. And they both got on well with Emma Downes, Megan's four year old. Emma was sometimes a little bossy. Six months older than the other two, she tended to lord it over them on occasion. But she loved them both. It shone out of her eyes each morning when she greeted them at the centre, and was apparent in the chattering talk that went on in the three toddler's seats fixed in the back of whichever car it was that came to pick them up in the afternoons, promptly at 4.00 PM.

Megan, Suzanne and Janie had met at the supermarket, of all places, one busy morning in Clarendon Street. Suzanne was reaching for a packet of jelly crystals above her head. Five- foot in flat shoes, and at the most five foot two in heels, she was having little success and had begun to cast her eye speculatively on the shelf above the floor. Would it take her weight if she jerked herself up on it? It was holding a great deal of weight now: large plastic bottles, at least twelve inches in diameter, full of orange and pineapple and bright lime green cordial, stood on it, six deep. She looked around. Would anybody notice? Would an officious floorwalker descend upon her, ordering her "off the furniture"? Should she look for a floorwalker to ask him to help? It usually was "him"; those jobs seemed to be reserved for men, while "checkout chicks" were women – or "girls" as they were no doubt referred to in the supermarket world. As she and others had been in the world of the bank. She riled at the thought. Why did they have to build the shelves so high, put jelly way up there, for God's sake?

"Need a hand?" The brisk but friendly voice cut in from behind, down the aisle and at the shelves near a stack of cans. It was a tall woman, all of five feet nine inches, or ten. "I'm Megan Downes," she said, smiling, businesslike, concerned. "I see you're having a bit of trouble there. Which flavour? How many?" She looked enquiringly at Suzanne.

"Oh. Oh, thanks. Raspberry and a blackberry if you can. Two of the one, one of the other."

Suzanne stepped back, bending her head backwards so she could see the shelves and their contents. Thwack! Her ankle struck a supermarket trolley which was positioned in the middle of the aisle. "Oh, gosh. Dammit. Now I've snagged my pantyhose," she began. Another shopper, her face red, her arms spread out, came running.

Another tall one, thought Suzanne idly. Where are they all coming from? The pain of the collision was momentary. She patted the other woman's arm.

Janie Rowe, for it was Janie whose shopping trolley stood, abandoned, in the aisle, looked anxiously at her. "You sure you're okay?" Suzanne nodded. "Well, what about a quick cup of coffee as compensation. I'm dying for sustenance. What about a Danish pastry, too. Let's be really wicked."

Suzanne grinned. She was only too well acquainted with the perils of Clarendon Street coffee shops and delis. She had succumbed. So had Megan. And so began a friendship which included coffee afternoons regularly, mostly in each other's houses, and at times back in Clarendon Street, or else down in Albert Park or Port Melbourne. Occasionally they made their way into town, sometimes by tram; other times, Janie, or Suzanne, or Megan took the car into the city, the three of them squashed into the front seat, parking it in a Bourke or Collins Street parking station until they finished browsing around in town and left, just in time to collect Kate, Sam and Emma from childcare.

It worked out well. They liked each other. They found they had interests in common. They discovered similarities in their early lives. They noted that they had followed similar career paths. Secretarial school. Looking for something more, and going to Tech. (as it was for Megan), or the CAE (as did Janie), or making it to University, as a mature age student (as with Suzanne). Megan began with a business course. "How to set up and run your own business." Then she began working at Prestons, a large department store with hundreds of employees, in the payroll branch. She became a whizz on ledgers, then graduated to computers and whatever the most modern equipment in accounting came to be. Prestons kept up with it all, and she kept up along with Prestons. After she married Sandy, she kept her job. Until she became pregnant with Emma. A month before the birth, she left, fully intending to return some months later. But caring for a baby, then a growing toddler, was no easy matter. She walked around for months like a zombie. Waking for early morning feeds, then through the teething. She was exhausted. It was only now that Emma was in childcare, that she was beginning to recover her equilibrium, and ready to concentrate her energies on herself. In between times, that is. Sandy needed looking after. Emma was not perpetually in childcare. But her energy levels were recuperating. It was then she had walked into the supermarket, just in time to meet Suzanne, just in time to accept the coffee invitation from Janie.

Janie Rowe had decided on accounting, quite early on. She began work in an office, as one of the "girls". Quickly she became "right hand man" to the boss. He was an accountant, and it didn't take long for her to realise she could do the job too. Conscientiously, she studied the long columns of figures, and began taking books home from the office for reading at night. Janie's boss, Mr Mandelert, had done an MBA at Melbourne, long before it became fashionable for every aspiring businessperson to have one. He had kept his books, and was quite willing for Janie to study them. He even gave her a hand sometimes, when she had difficulty in working out the problems in the standard text, Anthony and Reece's *Accounting Texts and Cases*. She graduated to *Financial Management and Policy in Australia*, by van Horne, Nicol and Wright. She gained entry into the accounting course at the CAE, and was able to study part-time while continuing to work for Mr Mandelert. It took her five years, but she made it. Then, with her degree under her arm, she asked the boss for a reference, and applied for a position in the Australian Securities Commission. She got it. Then she met Tom Rowe. He was a police officer, seconded to the Commission to work in the corporate crime area. She was smitten.

Mature age entry to university was high on Suzanne Renfree's list of priorities. She took the secretarial stream at school. Her father had come through the Korean war. Only just. He was never really well, coughing and choking at regular intervals. She knew it was important to get out and get a paid job. Secretarial work was easy for her, and she knew she could make a success of it. She saw the potential. It could lead to something else. No reason why she should not be able, with her brains and good fortune, to make it into the executive suite. So she thought.

After five years working at top pitch, doing the boss' job, filling in for him when he was away, covering for him when he was there, she could see that her hopes of advancement were nil. She looked around. One morning she came across it in the *Herald Sun*. An advertisement for mature age students, without Higher School Certificate to apply for entry to Monash. All it needed was the nous to sit for a couple of examinations, write a paper, and present sensibly and competently in an interview. She telephoned for the application form. When it came she filled it in and sent it off. She sat the exams, wrote the paper, and did her stuff before three solemn-looking academics. She was in.

When she was accepted, she went through a period of sheer terror. How could she ever have imagined she could go to university? she admonished herself. What a fool to think she could actually cope in the hallowed halls of academe. It was all a terrible mistake. Error in the admission procedures, without any doubt. Her name had wrongly been put in the "passes" rather than the "fails". She waited for a followup letter to arrive:

"Sorry. We made a mistake. You got the wrong letter. The one you got was for Garry Sampson."

"*Your* letter went by mistake to Gerry Peters."

"We're now putting things right. We enclose a copy of your letter. We sincerely regret the slip up. It occurred by the regrettable error of office staff. We cannot welcome you as a mature age student to this University at this time. You may care to try again, next year."

"Yes," thought Suzanne. "Blame the office staff. Some poor young woman will get it in the neck. All because someone at the top's too lazy to do it right..."

But no second letter arrived. There was no error: office staff, administrative, executive, professorial or otherwise. The letter she received was no hoax. She was in. Whether she liked it or not, she had to follow through. Keeping her job at the bank, she enrolled in commerce, then in her second year thought about doing commerce/law. She began getting distinctions in company law. Trade practices. Tax. Mercantile law. And anything else she tried her hand at.

"What do you reckon?" asked Megan Downes, raising her eyes from her coffee cup to meet Suzanne's and Janie's. They were sitting taking their afternoon coffee at the Renfree house. They had been going back over their lives in the paidwork force, and discussing their studies. She took a sip of coffee and went on, "You've got commerce, and almost a law degree, Suzanne. Janie's got accounting. I've done business procedures and payroll calculations 'til I'm blue in the face. Surely with all this talent bubbling around this table, we've got something to give the world. How about it, *girls*? Show the boys a thing or two. Or really, just show ourselves. What do you reckon, Suzanne? Janie?"

"Yes," agreed Janie. "I've just got to get something I can use my brain on. Sam's a lovely kid, but when you get down to it, a woman's got to have something intellectual going on in her life. Can't spend all day thinking in 'kinder' terms. It was great when Tom was still at the Commission. He used to come home with all the stories of corporate raids, fun with the figures. We used to talk about the schemes those businessmen got up to. Honestly, you wouldn't read about it. Thousands – no, millions – of dollars twisted and turned, laundered and re-laundered, robbing Peter to pay Paul, and James to pay them both. Classic."

She paused, dabbing at a few crumbs of Danish pastry that had fallen from her plate to the smooth surface of the table.

"But now he's transferred into the Armed Robbery Squad... A promotion, of course. But it's taken away a lot of my fun. A lot of his, too, I suspect. But a man's got to get on, of course."

Her voice dropped. Suzanne covered her hand, comfortingly. "Don't worry, kid. We'll come up with something. All this talent just can't go to waste. We won't let it." Her eyes clouded over. She was thinking. Megan interrupted the silence.

"Well, we've just got to. I'm nearly going crazy, now, with just the house. Four walls to look at, apart from the times I do the shopping, and these afternoons. Sandy's okay. There he is, typical executive, working his way up the ladder. Still at Prestons. They've got him for life, I reckon. Dutifully controlling the payroll day in, day out. Thousands, maybe millions of dollars going through his hands each week. Staff increasing. Payroll increasing. Him getting more and more important by the day. Me gently going more and more insane by the week. It's got to stop!"

As she raised her voice, Suzanne sat up straight in her chair, taking a long sip of coffee. It was still hot, she noted. Good coffee pot, that one.

"You know, girls," she said, looking around the table, first at Janie, then at Megan.

"Not only do we have our own talent. Why, right here on tap we've got a whole wealth of knowledge about current payroll procedures; the whole banking industry, what with Nick working himself to death at head office now, responsible for all the city branches; and everything the police are doing, whatever they think is important, in the armed rob. industry."

It was quiet. Janie and Megan put down their cups so carefully that there was no sound of china chinking on china, cups clattering against sauces, tea spoons tinkling against the fine round bowls of paper thin porcelain. Suzanne looked up.

"What about a bit of creative accounting, girls?"

"Get everything okay?" Suzanne bent her head, leaning over to push the door wide so that Megan could climb into the car. "Fine, fine," said Megan, throwing several large, grey-green looking sacks in between the back of the front seats and the cushions of the rear seat. She chucked Sam under the chin. "How's it going, Sam? Emma? Kate? The three toddlers smiled and laughed, nodding gleefully from their highly perched carseats, fixed into Suzanne's car.

"Whew! Well, good work today," smiled Megan, settling herself into the car, snapping her seatbelt.

"No problems at all, really. Think we've got it down to a fine art, now. Can't get too cocky and spoil things by over-confidence, I know. But I think it's time for a real pat on the back for us all."

"Janie got off okay, then?" asked Suzanne.

Megan nodded assent. "Yes. Last I saw of her, she was jumping (elegantly, of course; always elegant, our Janie) on to the No. 12 tram. Good idea to try Collins Street, this time. Less distance to go before getting on, and it'll take her almost home."

As was usual on these afternoons, Suzanne had been on time. She had kept the motor idling while she waited for Megan, and now she let in the clutch and drew out from the kerb. Behind them, she could see in the rearvision mirror something of a commotion breaking out all along the top of Collins Street, just up from the corner where she had waited for Megan. The police sirens were growing louder, and the crowd milling around on the footpath in front of the bank, to the rear and across the way, was growing larger. Several bank officials appeared on the front steps, and a security guard dressed in grey was peering out from behind one of the doors. She accelerated, driving down the hill toward Spencer Street and the Kingsway overpass. Soon, they would be in South Melbourne, and home.

"Not a bad haul," said Suzanne. It was several months and a number of fast manoeuvres later. She patted three large packages which were sitting on the table, one in front of each of them, and grinned. She took a sip of coffee, then a bite of Danish pastry, then looked up at Janie and Megan. "Hey, look at this. The papers just don't know what to say. Nor do the police, it seems." She indicated the front page of the *Herald Sun*, jabbing at it with her finger:

> Detective Tom Rowe of the Armed Robbery Squad said today the police are baffled by the series of payroll raids carried out on banks in the city area over the last six months. He called on anyone who might know anything to come forward.
>
> 'It's clear this gang has considerable backup and support, somewhere,' Detective Rowe said. 'There are just no leads. We've checked and rechecked all known gangs and individuals with a record in these areas, without any luck.'
>
> He told a packed press conference called by the Commissioner of Police that it was time some civic minded member of the community who had any information at all gave it to police. 'Someone must know something,' he told the thirty or so assembled reporters, journalists and television crew. 'There's never been a case in Victoria before just like this. Usually, they

slip up somewhere. If there's someone who's harbouring these men, we ask them to come forward and we will give them all the protection they need. If they're being threatened, it's better for them to come forward. We'll maintain all confidentiality.'

The police are working overtime on the case. Detective Rowe said they are in contact with police interstate and are searching through the files of known armed robbers, particularly from Sydney and Brisbane, to determine whether the *modus operandi* fits with any known interstate gang. He told the press conference that no details about the getaway car had been recorded by anyone near the scene of any of the raids. 'It's as if they vanish into thin air, everytime,' he added."

"Poor Tom," sighed Janie. "I really worry about him and that job. They've added five extras to the squad, and they're talking about calling in three from Sydney and two from Queensland. Of course it's giving them a bit of leverage with the government, what with demands for extra funding for more police, but it's also putting them in the pooh a bit in that department as well. Tom says the government can say: 'What the hell. You never catch them anyway. Can't do it with what you've got, you're not going to do it with more.' They're really worried down at headquarters, I can tell you."

"Yes," nodded Suzanne. "I think the pressure's on all right. And it's not only the government and opposition who're jumping up and down about law'n'order. The banks are getting at them, too, I hear."

"And the companies," said Megan, sinking back into her chair from where she had been reading the *Herald Sun* report from over Suzanne's shoulder. "Sandy says Prestons are livid about losing three payrolls all in the space of six weeks. And Anderson and Co., and Metro-Mainliners are furious as well. They've joined forces, in a way. Holding meetings in the bunker – well, the offices at Prestons. Management has decided the police can't do a thing right, so they're trying to build in 'robbery free' procedures. Consulting with each other every Wednesday, now, because Thursday's payday, and seems to be the trouble spot."

"Well, I guess they might find there is no real pattern, pretty soon," said Suzanne. "The summer sales are coming up, and we all know what happens then. Why, anyone does. Anyone who does any shopping, pays any attention to the sales' advertisements."

"And who reads the stories about the million dollar turnovers all the stores have – especially at the sales," interrupted Megan.

"Scads of people just crowding in the doors, anxious to spend, spend, spend. Relieve themselves of money well earned. Frantic to get rid of it," exclaimed Janie.

"And it all goes into the tills at Prestons, and Robert Martins, and Studley & Son..." added Suzanne.

"And then they have to add it up, record it, deliver it to the banks..." put in Megan.

"Any gang would have to take that into account," smiled Suzanne. "Can't depend on payrolls for ever, you know. They should know." She laughed. "But will the shops and the banks and the cops be ahead of this terribly, terribly difficult gang of three, or will they be behind them?"

"Way behind them, that's my intelligence." Janie laughed. Suzanne and Megan joined her.

"Well," said Megan shortly. "What are we sitting here for. Get out the pads and pencils. It's planning time. And keep an eye on the clock. It's my turn to collect the kids today."

In July the papers were full of it, still. "Armed Robbery Gang Remains At Large" screamed the headlines. "Police *Still* Baffled," they ran. "Commissioner Declares His Men on the Ball." "Banks Call for Increased Security Measures." "Interpol Called In."

Serious television journalists, looking down their noses, were told by their producers to elevate the story to the lead in news broadcasts. The *Financial Review*, hardly likely to devote its pages to bank robberies, took up the tale, taking the monetary losses from banks and business as the key. No one could turn on a radio talkback programme without hearing someone going on about the "gang of three". There was a lot of moralising. And a grudging respect.

Two men, only, had ever been sighted. About 5' 9" and 5' 10" in height, went the sightings. Stockings over their heads. ("Pantyhose, these days," said the police.) Slim, wiry build.

Hair colour – sometimes seemed to be dark, sometimes light. Could be dyed. Could be wigs. Clothes – ordinary. Work-a-day jeans, brown shoes, possibly sneakers. Checkered jackets sometimes. Sometimes windcheaters. Sometimes light, terylene-type overcoats. But there had to be a third. The one who had never been seen. There had to be a driver of a getaway car. Even if that had never been seen, either. How else could they get away from the scene so quickly? Couldn't see them boarding a tram in Swanston Street, laughed the police to themselves. On the rare occasions they now laughed, when armed robberies were mentioned. On the rare occasions they laughed at all.

Megan and Janie and Suzanne received daily updates, now, from their respective spouses, on the business. Janie got regular police bulletins. Megan heard nightly of Prestons taking the lead in devising foolproof controls in liaison with the banks. When "foolproof" was found wanting, she heard of *more* new steps. Suzanne, ever the good wife, listened avidly as Nick mused over the evening meal and later, as they were undressing for bed, on bank security and "extraordinary measures" becoming routine.

The streets buzzed with it, too. It was on the lips of the shoppers at the supermarkets, and the delis and coffee shops in Clarendon Street. And Albert Park. And Port Melbourne. (And elsewhere, no doubt, thought the three, when they got together at their regular coffee afternoons.

It was one such afternoon in September. The sun shone brightly in a blue sky. A light breeze was blowing. It was a perfect spring day. Megan looked at Janie, Janie looked at Suzanne, as they sat in Suzanne's kitchen, sipping coffee from the percolator and eating Danish pastries.

"You know, comrades, maybe it's time to do a once over, a review of the year's activities," she said. "Emma's not getting any younger. She's off to school in February. No more Russell Street childcare for her. No more daily pickups of Emma together with your Sam and Kate." She paused. "I've been thinking. Maybe it's time to think long term. Get into some long range planning. They were always going on about that at tech. 'Sort out your priorities. Think longterm.' It's not a bad idea…"

Suzanne chipped in, her face going slightly pink. "Yes, I think you're right, Megan. Kate'll be off to school before long, too."

"And so will Sam," added Janie. "And – and – Megan. Suzanne. I've got some news. I'm – I'm pregnant. I waited until I was really sure. I'm four months. The date's early February, according to the mid-wife. I – we – thought it was about time Sam had a sister. Or brother, I guess."

Megan and Suzanne began speaking at once. They stopped. Megan bowed her head slightly in deference to Suzanne. Suzanne bowed hers to Megan. They began, together, again.

"I'm having one…"

"Me, too…"

They collapsed into laughter, all three together. When they had recovered, they settled themselves in their chairs, coffee cups firmly in their hands, Danish pastries lying delicately, one on each plate.

Suzanne spoke first. "Long range planning, you were saying, Megan. Sounds as if we're already into it. What say we take a year or so off. Maybe eighteen months." She paused. "Kate, Sam and Emma will be well and truly settled into school by then. And we'll have Tom and Ned and Alice…Or Luke, Grace and Fran…All twelve or so months old, making their way in the world. We'll have time on our hands, again."

"True, true," said Janie. "And in the interim, we can plan – well, we can plan what we like, keep up with the latest in police tactics and advances, police detection methods. Take account of developments in the banking industry. Keep tabs on payroll calculations and department store security polices and procedures."

Suzanne indicated her agreement. Megan nodded assent. They sipped their coffee and nibbled at their pastries.

Suddenly, Suzanne glanced at her watch. "Goodness me! Get with it, *girls*. It's off to the centre. Got to collect Kate, Emma and Sam. They'll be waiting if we don't hurry it." She leapt up, gathering up her handbag which was on the spare chair, near the sink.

"And, *girls*." She paused. "You know me, with my height. Or rather, without it. I've got to have something to do in eighteen months time, too. *I've* picked the kids up promptly on the dot, brought them with me to the appointed pickup place always on time. Essential to the team work. Can't spoil that record."

She went toward the door, Janie and Megan, towering over her, in her wake. She turned:

"If we get to Russell Street a few minutes before four, we can talk to Ms Costain about her prospective new charges. Can't have Tom and Ned and Alice...or Luke, Grace and Franny...missing out on a place, not when it'll be so vital to their well being – and our – longterm...business...careers."

Megan, Janie and Suzanne hurried toward the car, a car of indifferent make (though mechanically sound, as they made sure), nondescript colour, and so sturdily domestic a presence. As they climbed in, companionably squashed together in the front seat, they might have been saying to one another, long range plans to the fore, "It's never too early to enrol the little ones in childcare."

Laxettes

"COME ON, GAYLEENE, look dumb. Get into the part. You're a girl who's never seen a spanner or a hinge. You haven't a clue what a screwdriver looks like, much less which end goes where. You don't know what a bevelled edge is. Haven't any idea what a chisel is. You can't do it. You c-a-n't do it. You need help. You're never going to be able to put that hinge on that door without help. You *need* Wayne. You *need* him, baby. Gayleene. This is your big moment. You look up at him. He notices you struggling with the bit of wood and the door and the hinge and the screwdriver. You're dropping screws on the floor. You've been struggling for about ten minutes. You're about to cry. Come on, baby, let those big, big tears well-up in those big, big eyes of yours…That's it. That's it. Let them n-e-a-r-l-y spill over. N-e-arly, baby, but not quite. Can't have the mascara getting mucked up, you know…"

On the set at the regular three-day weekly filming of the daytime soapie *Life on Macartney Street*, Gayleene Melbourne wrestled with wood, door, hinge and bracket. She gazed up, across the workbench, into Wayne Gift's eyes. He was looking at her. He was coming over. He reached down and held the wood and the screws and the hinge and the door. He took up the bracket. He smiled. She was sure he was smiling at her, a warm, friendly smile. He gently took the screwdriver from her hand and, reaching down, solemnly and silently began marking the place where the hinge had to go, where the screws had to go in. From under her lashes, she looked up adoringly at him.

"Cut! Cut! Perfect Gayleene. You got that just right. Now Wayne. Put some sex into that screwdriver. Not too obvious.

This is a family show. But get the message across that you want this girl. You really want her. You don't care that here she is, sashaying into your domain, trying to take over carpentry and joinery. You know she can't do it. You know you're still king. She's dying for you to show her how. You are *it,* man. You are t-h-e best. No one ever got a hinge on the door with that great style you're showing now. She loves it. She loves it. She's about to fall into your arms. You've got her out of the mess. You're Davey Crocket and Superman and Michael Hutchence and Rob Lowe all rolled up in one…Well, okay, you're Wayne – Wayne – Wayne. Wayne Gift!"

Gayleene Melbourne and Wayne Gift were the great new duo of stage and screen. Well, it was the television screen, but who knew where it might lead to. They had begun working together as Tracey Medlow and Justin Smithson, the youngest of the cast of *Life,* as it had come to be known. For some reason they were attractive to the audience out there. Before they knew what had happened to them, *TV Weekend* had done major stories, splashed their pictures over the front cover and advertising billboards. *Television Today* followed up with centrespreads: a portrait photograph of Gayleene on one side, a picture portrait of Wayne on the other, and in the middle, Gayleene and Wayne together, their feet pointing at the right hand edge of the page, their blonde heads, haloed with sparking lights and a neighbourly closeness combined with a sensuality that sent the clear message: the kids next-door, the kids Mum and Dad can feel happy about, even if daughter Cheryl has the poster plastered on the wall with blue-tack so it marks the paint; even if son Adam or Jason has it secreted in the drawer by the bed. Even if you have a faint suspicion that daughter Kylie might have her head full of Wayne Gift when she's supposed to be doing her homework. Even if you catch young Darren lying on the bed, gazing dreamily into space, Gayleene and Wayne lying on the counterpane next to him, or stuffing the picture guiltily under his pillow, his face slightly red. After all, it's better, in the end, if Cheryl and Adam and Kylie and Darren and Jason are *inside,* and just having fantasies, rather than *outside,* with the realities: out there in the pinball parlours with the computer games or worse, up a back alley with a syringe, shooting-up. Families felt secure with Gayleene and Wayne.

Gayleene and Wayne (aka Tracey Medlow and Justin Smithson) were on their way. Millions of boys and girls around Australia actually *dreamt* of being Gayleene and Wayne. Even parents, feeling over the hill at thirty-five and forty, dreamt themselves back to teenagehood, surviving into next week on the strength of forgetting their stomachs were sagging, their breath getting short, their partner's hair falling out, the ravages of time creeping up and making them realise their own mortality.

At least, this was how the producers of *Life in Macartney Street* thought it was. They forgot that the media makes stars. That the media makes people out there "want" this week's Gayleene Melbourne and Wayne Gift. If the media latched on to Suzie May Jepson and Darryl Meggers, starring on the rival station's *On the Met*, the posters, the sweatshirts, the sneakers, the chocolate bars, the usual hype (or claptrap) of the sellable personality would churn out of the factories and shops. They forgot the force of the machine. That if that's all the public gets, in the end the public forgets it wants anything else.

Gayleene Melbourne hadn't forgotten, however. Gayleene Melbourne wanted something else. No, she certainly didn't mind the attention and the thrill that went with it, of knowing you were important – at least for today. As for tomorrow, what then? Gayleene thought about it often. Contrary to the way she was depicted in the movieguides and "low down on the soapies, and the stars you live with," Gayleene was not a dope. Gayleene wanted more. She wanted to be taken seriously. She boiled inside when Trevor Connington told her to "look dumb". She wasn't dumb. And she didn't really believe her character, Tracey Medlow of 62 Macartney St, was dumb either. She was intelligent, witty, independent, smart. How else had she, Gayleene Melbourne, ended up (begun, rather) as a famous star with a million fans, a huge following, at merely eighteen years and nine-and-a-half months? How else had Tracey, her alter ego, got a carpentry and joinery apprenticeship in the first place, anyway? It took guts to go into a field where women hadn't been before. And they wouldn't have let her in if she couldn't put a hinge on a door, as Trev was so busy telling her she couldn't. "Play dumb. Flutter your eyelashes. Look stupid, stupid." She'd give him "stupid". She'd give him "dumb". Tracy-Gayleene wasn't going along with that falsified picture of herself any more. So just you wait. Trev. Wayne.

"Okay. Cut. Coffee break."

The women members of cast and crew moved over to the sink and the urn and the cups and the milk and the tea bags and biscuits. Dutifully, they took down the cups, rinsing them under the hot tap and giving them a cursory whisk around with the teatowel that Jo, the "girl Friday" (as they continued to call it, despite the *Equal Opportunity Act* and the *Anti-Discrimination Act* and the *Sex Discrimination Act*, and affirmative action, and sexual harassment...), took home every night, washing and ironing (yes, ironing), bringing it back to be used by the women next day.

Gayleene banged a few cups about to relieve the tension that always seemed to arise, now, when she was on set with Wayne. She had noticed that it was when she was with Wayne that Trev made his usual demand for her bimbo look, to play the dumb broad. When she did scenes with her mother, or with other women in the cast, Trev forgot about making her look stupid. It was getting worse. She didn't know how long she could put up with it. Consciously drawing her shoulders back and raising her head high, she put coffee into two cups and filled them with hot water from the urn. Wayne took loads of milk and loads of sugar. She put them in, then reached into her pocket. Quickly, she scrabbled at the silver foil package that glittered and shone in her hand. She stirred Wayne's cup vigorously, dropping the scrunched up foil into the waste disposal unit to be mixed, in that churning, clanking motion of the new technology, into a glutinous mass of wet tea bags, old coffee grounds, and soggy indescribables. Then she turned to face the group that was sitting sprawled around the set, some lounging on the workbench where Tracey Medlow had played the superb scene of young-woman-with-french-fries-for-brains. She took the cup over to Wayne. He took it without even noticing her. He kept talking to Johnno, one of the camera operators.

"Okay, kids. Back on set. Chop. Chop. We haven't got all the time in the world, you know, kiddies. Back to the grindstone." Trevor Connington was ready to go. As director-producer, his word went. They chop, chopped.

"Now, come on Wayne, get you're act together. This is your big scene, now. You're gazing at Gayleene. You've fixed her hinge on the door. You've helped her get top marks.

"Of course, your marks are the very top. She comes in second or third.

"Now, she's grateful. She's glowing all over with gratitude. You…"

Wayne looked pale. He grabbed Gayleene by the arm. Swayed. Took a few staggering steps. Then he ran. Ignoring the cameras, ignoring Trev, forgetting that he was Wayne Gift, media king, king of the teenyboppers, favourite of the Mums and the Dads, he plunged off the set and into the wings. The set was silent. Suddenly there was a thud. Ker-thud. The door of the Men's closed.

"Well, what the hell was all that about," grumbled Trevor Connington. "Dave. Get after him," he ordered the nearest man. "Get in there and see what he's up to. Get him out here AT ONCE."

Trevor was roaring. Who was Wayne Gift – Wayne Gift, I ask you – to ignore his orders like that? Ignore his direction? Treat him like a no one on his own set? This was *his* set. Trevor Connington's set. He hadn't got here by sitting around loafing, running off to the loo when the fancy took him. He, Trevor Connington, got here by sheer hard work. He was in charge. Some little pip-squeak of a Wayne Gift, however famous the magazines made him, wasn't going to get away with this…

Trevor fumed. Gayleene sat calmly at the workbench. Dave came back shuffling his feet and looking embarrassed. "It sounds as if he'll be there for a while, I guess. Making an awful noise, but he says he'll survive. Said we should get on with it and do another scene. Says he just can't come back on set yet. Impossible. I'd say he's right," said Dave, beginning to snigger.

"Okay, okay, back on set. Gayleene. We'll just have to play that again. Can't wait for Wayne to grace the screen with his presence again. Now, how can we work this. You've got to get that hinge on the door somehow. This is the big moment. You're parents are coming to the College "open day" tonight. Okay, Wayne's a fizzer. Try getting the thing on yourself, love. We'll just have to improvise. Look into the camera. Eyes big. That's right. Big, big eyes. You're doing it. You're getting the hinge on to the door. You're mastering it. You know where the screws go. It's all coming to you. It's as if you've had a revelation. It's all falling into place. Come on love, you can do it, you can do it."

She could. Gayleene Melbourne fixed the hinge to the door in exemplary fashion and looked straight up at the camera, a look of triumph on her face. Her face glowed. Trev's glowed too.

"*Terrific!* baby. That'll really knock 'em in the aisles... well, into their lounge chairs. That look is superb. We could get a big glossy out of that. Get the message upstairs, Dave, that we want that one made up as a still...Well, okay kids. That's it for today. Thanks for the good work. See you all Tuesday... And Dave, get in there and tell that Wayne he'd better have his act together next time. We can't afford to put up with the stars getting temperamental, however big they are, or think they are, and whatever the problem. Tell him."

Shirley Bonnington played Gayleene Melbourne's Mum in *Life on Macartney Street*. She had been an actor for as long as she could remember. God! It was hard in the early years, she thought. Hopeless parts for women, if there were any at all. The men managed to get themselves the best roles, which was only to be expected, because it was men playwrights who got

their plays accepted, workshopped, published. She remembered
the 1950s when Oriel Gray's grand play *The Torrents* shared
equal first prize with *The Summer of the Seventeenth Doll*. And
who had ever heard of *The Torrents* now? Oh, sure, she had.
And other women in the industry. But the public? No way. Ray
Lawler? *The Doll*? Everyone knew that. But Oriel Gray? Who
the hell was she?

The lighting on her mirror hid the wrinkles and the crêpiness
of her neck. She had arranged it that way about ten years ago,
when she saw time creeping up on her and knew that she
wouldn't last much longer in this game. A game for the young,
if you were a woman. And if you weren't young, you kept
pretending you were...

Well, no point in sitting around bitching at this time of life,
she thought. Better get the act together and make it to the set of
Life. She was getting sick of Trev telling her that her soapie
husband Herb had all the brains, and that she didn't have to say
or do anything much. "Just look like Tracey-Gayleene's Mum,"
he would say with a smirk. At least, she thought it was a smirk.
Probably, though, that was uncharitable. He couldn't help how
he looked. And it wouldn't even occur to him that there was
anything to smirk about in telling a woman that "just looking
like" someone's Mum meant they didn't have to do a thing.
Just exist. Sure, she existed. But she was fed up. She wanted a
role. She wanted to act.

"Okay, okay. All quiet on set. Johnno, get your camera angled
up here. I want a full-on of Shirley. Shirley, Dan's just told you
he's leaving you. You're shattered. You'll never get your life
together again. Your life is Dan. Okay, Okay, you've got Tracey,
sure. But what is a woman without a man, as they say in the
comics. You'll be lost without him. You won't know what to do
with yourself. You don't even know what money is, unless
you're spending it. You've never done a day's work in your life.
It's curtains for you, lady, what with Dan gone. Without Dan
Medlow, lady, *you are n-o-t-h-i-n-g*. NOTHING. Now, Shirley, go
for it...Oh, no, shit. Dan – Tom. What are you doing, man.
What's wrong?"

Tom Sorenson was swaying. He put down the coffee cup he had been holding, the remains of the recent coffee break.

The "girls" had fixed the coffee. Shirley, true to her character of "Tracey's Mum, Dan's Wife", had fixed Dan-Tom's coffee. Tom looked frantically at Trev. "Sorry, Trev. I just can't go on at the moment. Gotta go. Sorry..." He departed the set rapidly, clutching his stomach. Cast and crew heard the sound of a door closing somewhere back in the wings.

"Dave," yelled Trevor. Was that an answering moan?

"Okay, okay. Shirley. We'll have to go on without Dan. Can't wait. You people don't seem to realise that I've got to churn out three episodes of this sodding soapie a week. It-is-not-easy, let-me-tell-you. And particularly not with all this rushing off the set without warning. I don't know what's got into you people.

"Now Shirley. We'll have to play this differently. Let's get the scene together with Mary Oates. Mary, get yourself over here. You've got to be supportive of Shirley. Here she is, your oldest friend and neighbour. You've lived next door for thirty years. She's just told you that Dan's flipped out. He's running off with a twenty-five-year-old. What are you going to tell her? She'll survive? Okay, okay, play it your way. I've had this storyline. It's getting away from me.

"What, you say she can get him out of the house and stay living in Macartney Street; that she can keep the car and take over the bank accounts? Okay, okay ladies. You do want you want. Am I in charge or what? But roll the cameras..."

"No, no, no. I can't stomach this. I've let you play it your way, Shirley and Mary, but I cannot believe this. You can't have a family show where the wife actually starts running her own life and believes she might live when her husband tells her he's running off with a younger woman. She'd have to be shattered. Shirley, you-are-distraught. Now, Mary, pull yourself together. Get back to your lines. This is not anarchy week...it's not...what's that? Oh, thanks Dorrita, that's just what I need. I always knew you'd make a superb Assistant Director, always with a cup of coffee on hand when the brains of the operation needs it. Oooh. That's GOOD. Okay, kids, let's take a short break, and you get your act together, Shirley. You-are-the-shattered-wife."

"Right. Back on set. We're ready to roll. Shirley, you're sitting with your head in your hands, make your shoulders shake and get ready to look up at your old friend Mary, with your mascara running down your cheeks. You're a sad and sorry sight, Shirley, no wonder Dan's leaving you – left you. You are distraught. Gayleene, you get ready to come in. Your mother's falling apart. Your world's going to pieces...Get moving, get mov...Ye Gods! Get me off this set. Get out of my way. Stan, move. Johnno, don't stand there gawking. Dave, get out of my way. Get-out-of-my-way!"

Trevor Connington plunged, his face red and perspiring, hastily to the left. The crews' eyes followed him, amazed. This was the first time in what seemed a lifetime that they had ever seen Trevor leave the filming of any project he had been on. That wasn't his style. He exercised total control. He had total control. This just wasn't like Trevor Connington.

They heard a door open rapidly, then close, ker-thunk. There was a rushing sound of air as the rubber surrounds of the doorjamb connected with the frame. The large, oldfashioned sign "Gents" stood out starkly, painted black against the white door. The men looked at each other and shrugged their shoulders.

Shirley Bonnington looked at Mary. Mary looked at Gayleene Melbourne. Gayleene looked at Shirley, then looked at Dorrita. Dorrita Elms, Assistant-Director, cum Director, looked at the three other women. "Okay, *girls*, get on with it," she yelled.

"Boys, get back up there, on those cameras. Focus, focus. I want a direct camera line on Shirley as Gayleene comes in the door. Gayleene, you're smiling. You're seeing your Mum come alive for the first time in twenty years. She's actually starting to live. Okay, boys, lights, camera, film rolling. Come on boys, get to work. You've got a team of women working here, and we mean business."

Getting the Message

IT WAS NOTORIOUS amongst his staff that Mr Andreoni was a sexual harasser and a peeper. Sometimes, Tania and Mercy thought this was the only reason he had set up shop in the fashion industry: an opportunity to get his sweaty hands on the female shop assistants who were employed to sell clothes to women, and an opening for him to spy on his customers. And "opening" was right. Tania had often suspected there was a reason for the dressing cubicles being positioned as they were, rear walls fronting on to the area where Mr Andreoni sat doing his office work (and where staff were forbidden to tread). Well, ostensibly doing his office work. It was Mercy who discovered the peepholes cleverly concealed behind the mirrors. She reported it to Tania with distress and distaste, a distaste that rose to fury when the two of them went out to lunch, sitting in a nearby coffee lounge, to discuss the whole business.

"It's really just too bad of him. Probably been going on for years. And what are we going to do about it," asked Mercy firmly. "We can't let it go on now that we know for sure."

"Yes," agreed Tania. "It was bad enough when he was all fingers and thumbs and hands and slimy slobber over us, but I guess we could cope with that. Though why we should..." Her voice trailed off, then she came back to the conversation. "But peeking through holes in the walls at undressed women just tops the lot."

Tania Siddons was twenty-two. She wanted to make a name for herself in the fashion world. After finishing school, she had gone to East Sydney Tech to learn fashion design, graduating with high marks and great promise. But just as actors don't necessarily get parts, however good they might be, so dress designers are not necessarily snapped up by fashion houses looking for new talent. Rather than join the dole queue, Tania applied for jobs wherever she thought she could build on her expertise. Eventually, it came to selling clothes, rather than designing them. But she took it in good part. Heavens! Even if she ran her own design company (as she intended for the future), she would have to engage in selling. No point in having ideas if you couldn't get other people to buy them. And she wanted to see "her" clothes walking around the Sydney streets – and Melbourne, and Brisbane, Adelaide, Perth, New York, London! She buckled down to working hard at understanding the female psyche and how to cater to women's picture of themselves, how to positively enhance that picture rather than detract from it.

Andreoni's Fashion Boutique was the sixth shop Tania tried. She had almost despaired with walking the streets, wearing the soles off her shoes as her father would have said. Then she got the job, though she didn't like Mr Andreoni at all, right from the start. But she needed a job. And this *was* a job. She looked around at the clothes racks, row upon row of the latest fashions, day wear, evening wear, elegant, dressy, some more in the teen-scene line. If only she could ignore the boss, she thought, she could survive here well.

Mercy Adamson was already there. She came into the business with very different credentials. Tall, lithe, youthful-looking, at twenty-six she had almost despaired of "making it" as a top-class model. To be honest with herself, she had to admit she hadn't really made it to first base. Tried everything: right modelling school, great pics in a professional looking portfolio, perfect dress-sense, always well displayed. But somehow, she just didn't click. Not the right "look" for the '80s, she gathered. Had to look twelve rather than nineteen, and once over twenty, a woman was in a real disaster area. She outwardly settled for selling clothes rather than modelling them and making her mark in New York, Europe, London. The fashion capitals. Face on the cover of *Vogue*. A woman had to eat.

Mercy ate, courtesy of the low wages paid by Mr Andreoni, and merely clenched her teeth when he came near her, then slid away, out of his grasp, and off to the other side of the shop where she fussed about elegantly among the racks, smoothing the garments on their broad plastic hangers, or brushing lint from suit collars.

Mercy Adamson and Tania Siddons swiftly became friends. Each appreciated the other's aspirations. Each supported the other in her work. Each did her best to "be there" whenever Mr Andreoni was on the prowl, so that the shop was never left single-staffed, one of the women alone with him. Saturdays and Thursday and Friday late night shopping were easiest to cope. There always seemed to be customers in the shop, and two or three other staff came in to work special hours. Dacey Manners was a regular, making enough to keep herself at East Sydney Tech while she finished her designer course. Tania had known her vaguely when she was going through, although she was a year or so ahead. Dacey was only seventeen, and Mercy and Tania were particularly careful to ensure they were nearby whenever she was in the shop and Mr Andreoni was about.

The day after the council of war at the Medieval Coffee Lounge near Castlereagh Street, Dacey Manners came to Tania, almost in tears. Mr Andreoni had managed to get her alone in one of the cubicles when the others were busy with their customers. On the excuse of admonishing her for her appearance and charging that her hem was rucked up at the back, he had slipped his hand up her dress and touched the top of her thigh. Fortunately, Dacey told them, she had leapt out of the way, more in shock than anything else, and he had tripped and fallen against the stool near the mirror in the dressingroom. She had taken advantage of his momentary lack of balance, and fled between the curtains.

Now, she came to them asking what to do. Couldn't leave the job. She was locked in to paying the rent on a very humble room in Darlinghurst Road. She, like Mercy and Tania, had to eat. Jobs were not easy to get these days. How did they survive, working all day with Mr Andreoni lurking about? If they managed, surely she could manage too?

"It's not enough just sitting here and grumbling about him," said Mercy to the other two. Now the three of them were sitting around a table at the Medieval Coffee Lounge. "We've got to stop him, or leave, or maybe do both."

"But we can't just up and leave with the rent unpaid, fares to cover, Dacey's school stuff, and my drawing equipment, always going up in price," returned Tania. "I just can't leave my designing to one side while I keep myself together earning money in that dress shop. I've got to keep it up. Don't you want to keep up your aerobics, and our good times out once in a blue moon?"

Mercy nodded her acquiesence. "But we can't just leave it at that. Got to do more." She frowned, her forehead crinkling slightly, and ran her hand through her hair. "Think, women, think!"

Tech was on holidays. Dacey was working during the week to make some extra money to cover her expenses. It was Saturday, 4.30 PM closing. Dacey glanced at Mercy for the signal. Tania created a diversion, asking Mr Andreoni to come over to look at the display in the window. In skilful co-ordination, Dacey swooped to the front of the shop and closed the large, single shutter firmly, and Mercy slid out to the back, to Mr Andreoni's office. The telephone in the front of the shop had already been disconnected, the plug plucked from its socket by Tania a short time earlier, the phone piece itself secreted at the bottom of the bin that held discarded hangers. He would never find it there. Nor would he find his office telephone. Mercy flicked it from the fixture that held it and, scooping the instrument up in her arms, dashed quickly back into the shop. Depositing it in the space under the till at the front counter and shoving some plastic bags over it to conceal it, she picked up one half of a plastic hanger that had been broken in two, in preparation the evening before.

Mr Andreoni was just now turning from the window. He began to move back, towards the office area. Tania hovered at his elbow and Dacey was standing over on the left, moving up toward him on his right hand side. Mercy walked around the counter, veering towards the evening racks which formed a heavy shield between Mr Andreoni and the window. Waiting for him to pass her, Mercy flicked a St Laurent scarf, brightly coloured in the reds and blacks of the season, around the broken hanger she held in her hand. Just as he walked by, Mercy pivoted on her right heel and came up directly behind him. Thrusting the rounded end of the hanger into the small of his back she hissed in his ear, "Okay, mate. Get 'em up."

Startled, Mr Andreoni stumbled, almost falling against Tania who quickly leapt out of the way. He recovered his stride, and glanced to his left. Dacey stood, too far for him to grab her and use her as a shield, but close enough for him to know, by the expression on her face, that he could expect no help from her. He looked to his right. Tania's face was flat and closed. No help there.

"What are you..." he garbled, playing for time. "Get 'em up," the voice repeated.

It had to be Mercy. Couldn't be anyone else. What was this? What was going on? He took a tentative step forward, then tried to move, gently, slowly, across to the door. "Stop right there," said Mercy sharply. "I mean it. We're not playing games."

Clearly, they were all in it. And what was "it"? He put up his hands and resigned himself to doing as he was told. It was three against one. He had no chance.

It was humiliating, Mr Andreoni thought as he tugged the thin grey blanket more firmly around his shoulders. His naked shoulders. He could hardly bear to think about the situation in which he now found himself, courtesy of "those women".

After directing him towards his office, Mercy Adamson had demanded he remove his clothing. When he had hesitated, she had shoved him harder in the back with what he knew was a gun. Tania Siddons had added her voice, too. He had no choice. Even that young one, Dacey Manners, looked menacingly at him when he turned his head slightly in an effort to persuade them they shouldn't be treating him in this way. What had *he* ever done to *them*? He had reluctantly removed his suit jacket and tie, thinking that would satisfy them. It didn't. He took off his shirt. Surely that was sufficient? Slowly, he began unbuckling his belt.

The pile of clothing on his desk rose correspondingly with the growing nakedness of his body. It was cold and he was beginning to grow a little frightened. What would they do to him next?

One of the voices kept telling him to "move it". In his growing terror he was now unable to distinguish between them. Women's voices, that was all he knew. Oh, God! If only he hadn't set himself up in a women's business. He didn't want to see a woman ever again. If he survived all this he would – he would –

"Come on, get on with it." The voice broke in. He let his trousers fall to his ankles. "Get them off." His hands shaking, he pulled the legs over his feet, and added the pants to the pile on the desk.

"Okay, stick this blanket around yourself, and get the underpants off. And quickly." He felt, rather than saw, a folded, grey-looking blanket fall beside him on the ground near where he stood. He stooped to pick it up.

"We've got no desire to see you in the flesh, Andreoni. Can't think of anything less edifying. But just get on with it, man. And take off the watch as well, while you're at it."

At last, he had done as they demanded. His clothes sat in a neat, folded pile, the watch (worth $1,000; it went fleetingly through his mind that he should at least fight to keep that) perched on top. The blanket was wrapped around his bare skin.

And now, here he sat, cold and alone, in his office. After he had undressed, they had taken his clothes away and locked the door. But first, they set on a table a bowl of warm water and a packet of plaster of paris.

"Get to work," one of them said. (Probably that Mercy; she was a real trouble maker, despite her ethereal looks, thought Mr Andreoni, slipping between rage and fear.) "You've got half an hour to get those peep holes into each of the dressing-rooms filled up, tight, so that you can't play Peeping Tom any more, Andreoni. Get to it."

"We'll be waiting outside, and we're going to inspect the job when you've finished," said another voice. (No doubt Tania this time, fumed Mr Andreoni; she was a sly one. Always avoiding him. No deference to him as the boss, that was her trouble. He should have got rid of her long ago.) "Just make sure you don't miss *any* holes. And they've got to be sealed tight."

The door slammed shut. He hesitated, then hurried over, grabbing at the handle. No luck! It was firmly locked. The deadlock he had installed was immoveable under his hand. The key, which he left in the lock when he was in the office, had been turned and taken away. They must have it. Those women. They had observed more of his habits than he thought. Almost sobbing with anger and anxiety, he fell back into the room, flopping into his expensive leather office chair.

Then he had thought of his gun. The gun he kept in the desk drawer against emergencies. In a business where there were likely to be large sums of money about, a man had to have protection. Thank goodness he had had such foresight as to arm himself. He pulled open the drawer. The gun lay in its usual place. Ha! Ha! Weren't as smart as they thought, these women. He had them. He'd shoot the lock off and scare the wits out of 'em.

Grabbing up the gun, he flicked open the chamber to check the bullets. It was empty. How can that be? he wondered, his eyes opening wide in amazement. It's always loaded, just in case. His hand fumbled in the drawer, towards the back where he kept the carton of cartridges. It wasn't there. It wasn't there!

And then, he realised what had happened. Those women had noticed even more about him than he ever knew. He had thought he never left his office unguarded. But then, a man has to pee once in a while. And he had had to go out into the back maze of passages, where the toilets, shared by all the shops in Centrepoint, were situated. Invariably, even on these occasions, he locked the office door. But he must have slipped up. And just once was enough. He thought back to when he last looked at the gun. Maybe a week ago, and even then he hadn't checked on whether or not it was loaded. Had just assumed it was, as always. He had no way of knowing when one of them had snuck in here and taken away – no, stolen, STOLEN, the bullets from the drawer, and emptied the gun.

He should have known there was something going on when each of them had resigned within about five days of each other, their resignations to take effect today, Saturday. Tania Siddons had come to him first. Some story about another job at a boutique right here in Centrepoint. Well, would he have something to say about that, now. Make a complaint to the manager. Put in a bad word. Then Dacey Manners had told him she didn't need the job any more. Left some money by a maiden aunt, so she didn't have to do any more part-time work. Was going to finish off her fashion designing course full-time, then set up her own business. He wouldn't let her get anywhere in the trade. He still had some connections. He'd use them and she'd get nowhere. And as for that Mercy Adamson. Thought she was going to be a top model! She'd never get anywhere, if he had anything to do with it. She'd never get another job selling clothes. Not even selling pizza. Thought she was going to join Tania in that other shop, did she? Well, he'd put a stop to it...as soon as he got out of here.

He rubbed his hand across his forehead. Although his body was cold, and he was even shivering, his face was sweating profusely. Well, he would have to telephone someone for help. He would just have to cope with their finding him here, without his clothes, overpowered by three silly women. Have to make up some sort of explanation. But he had to get out, whatever the short price of public exposure he had to suffer to escape. His hand reached for the telephone, and scrabbled at emptiness. It wasn't there. IT WASN'T THERE! The telephone was gone. He bent his head, looking down behind the desk. The telephone jack looked back at him. Or rather, the empty socket stared at him from the wall. He was almost sobbing, now.

After a few moments (though it could have been hours, he was losing his sense of time) he had realised that there was no point in just sitting. He had to get the plaster mixed and the peep holes filled. They had said half an hour. Maybe if he worked to time, they would let him out and that would be the end of it.

But that had been about an hour ago, he thought. It was difficult to judge the time, without his watch. What were they doing? Maybe they had just gone. Lit out and left him here. He didn't know whether to be pleased they had left him alone, or terrified they had abandoned him. How would he escape?

Slowly he got up from the chair, where he had been slumped against the desk, and crept over to the door. He pressed his ear against the panels, but could hear only silence. Bending down, he looked at the slight gap between the floor and the bottom of the door. Kneeling, he pressed his head against the floor, trying to see through, into the recesses of the shop. The gap was too small.

But then, he heard something. There was a slight rustle. He pressed himself against the floor again, manoeuvring his head so that his ear was closest to the streak of light that showed between the floor and the door. Rustling. Yes, there was definitely the sound of rustling. It was like – like paper…or plastic…or paper and plastic. What was it? He pressed his ear against the gap more firmly. At least it meant that he was not abandoned. They were still there. It had to be them, making the noise. What were they doing?

For an age, he retained the cramped position, head on the floor, ear squashed up against the hard edge of the door. But he was rewarded only with more rustles and a few soft words occasionally spoken by the three outside. At last, beaten, he limped back to his chair and placed his head in his hands, his elbows leaning leadenly on the desk. He was a sad, sad man.

Hours later, it seemed, Mr Andreoni crept back to the door. Just as he bent to press his ear once more against the crack, he was startled by a thump on the door.

"Just sitting around in there, Andreoni?" barked a voice. It was Mercy. Or Tania. Or even the shy, delicate Dacey as he had earlier thought of her. "We've nearly finished out here. Have you finished in there? If those holes aren't plugged up by the time we're through, you'd better watch out."

"They're finished, they're finished," Mr Andreoni almost sobbed as he leaned up against the door, pressing against it with all his weight, hoping that somehow it would fall away, and the door would be open, leading him out, out to freedom. But the door remained solid, cutting him off from the shop, from his clothes, from the street. But at least it was a barrier between himself and those women. Would they do anything more to him?

There was a slight noise from below, near his feet. He saw a piece of white paper nudging its way under the door. "Grab this, Andreoni. And read it. It's a confession, and you'd better sign it. We'll give you another half an hour."

He bent to pick up the proffered sheet. He found it was three pieces of paper, all one size, with an identical message neatly typed on each:

"I, Tomas P. Andreoni, proprietor and manager of Andreoni's Fashion Boutique, state that over the past six years of my proprietorship and management I have sexually harassed my staff. Over that same period I have also peeped into cubicles to observe customers in various states of undress. For this purpose, I drilled holes between the office and the dressingrooms, concealing them near the mirrors.

"I acknowledge that these practices are unlawful and contravene the provisions of the *Anti-Discrimination Act* and the *Sex Discrimination Act.*

"I acknowledge that I am liable for any loss, damage, pain and suffering caused to my current and former employees by my activities.

"I acknowledge that I am liable for any loss, damage, pain and suffering caused to customers trying on clothing in this shop, whether or not they purchased clothing from Andreoni Fashion Boutique.

"I undertake that I shall not in the future engage in these practices."

At the bottom of each sheet his name was typed, with a dotted line appearing immediately above it, and a space for him to sign. He took up his pen.

"Okay, Andreoni. You can pass those papers back, under the door. But only if you've signed, man. And if you haven't..."

The voice, menacing, paused. Hastily, he scrabbled his signature on each page. It was done. He got up, hurried over, and thrust the papers between the floor and the door. He heard someone grabbing them up. There was a pause. She — whichever one of them it was — was inspecting the signature.

"All right, seems okay." He could hear the voices, faintly, on the other side of the door. He pressed his ear against the panels.

"Well, Andreoni, hope you've learnt your lesson. If we hear of anything going on in this Boutique again — and we'll keep tabs on you, don't you worry — we'll take these to the Anti-Discrimination Board and take action against you." That sounded like Mercy Adamson.

Then Tania Siddons chimed in. "And we're leaving you a pile of reading matter out here on the front counter. All the decisions of the Equal Opportunity Tribunal and the Human Rights Commission where women have been awarded damages against employers like you, Andreoni. You'd better read them, and remember them."

"Yes, yes," he moaned. "But when am I going to get out of here? When are you going to let me out?"

"What's that, Andreoni? Want to get out? Are the holes plugged up yet?"

"Yes, yes, yes," he whispered into the panels of the door. "They're set dry."

"Well, we're not ready to let you out yet, so go back to your desk, sit down, and think some more about your conduct, Andreoni. We'll give you another half an hour."

There was a pause. Obediently, he returned to his chair. His head in his hands again, he heard the voices receding.

Outside, it was dark. The long shadows that fell from the windows, little more than airvents at the top of the back wall of Mr Andreoni's office, had been swallowed up. How many minutes or hours had passed, Mr Andreoni could not tell, but it was time, he thought, to turn on the light. He had to discover whether those wretched women were still about, or if they had gone off, leaving him naked and alone.

He rose, his feet cold on the linoleum floor and, feeling his way around the wall, staggered over to the door. He flicked the switch and the light flooded on, making him blink.

There had been no shaft of light from the crack under the door between office and shop when he stood up. Probably they had left. Mr Andreoni glanced down. It was then that he saw a corner of paper poking from under the door. Wearily, and clasping his hand on his right knee as he bent, he reached for it.

It was an envelope. As he tugged at it, he felt its weight and thickness. The key! Fingers trembling, he tore the seal. There was a piece of paper inside, wrapped around the key. Mr Andreoni crumpled it, then thrust the thin piece of metal into the lock – and turned it. It worked! He was free.

Before opening the door, he paused, looking down at the still crumpled paper in his left hand. He could see there was writing on it , and he smoothed it out, peering shortsightedly at the words. Sighing, he returned to the desk, perched his glasses on his nose, and sat once more in his chair.

"Mr Andreoni," he read, the name neatly typed at the head of the page. Underneath ran the message:

"By the time you read this, the shop will be empty of us. It's quite safe. You can come out. No one will be peeking at you, as you have so often peeked at others.

"Your clothes have been carefully packaged in a box together with the shop and office telephones. We're posting them as we go, on the way down to Wynyard. They'll be sent priority from the main post office, so (barring a mail strike) they'll be delivered here at the shop first thing Monday morning.

"There's a hamburger and french fries on the counter for dinner, and if you decide to wait for your suit, we've left three cans of baked beans, four bread rolls, three bananas and a can opener.

"Goodbye and good luck. And no more peeping.

"We know you wish us well."

It was not signed, but at the bottom appeared the slogan: "Fight Sexual Harassment", and the initials "D.M.T."

Below, they had typed a postscript:

"Don't think you can use this note in any way. We're sure you won't go to the police. You have too much to hide, don't you, Mr Andreoni? But it wouldn't help to show them this note. It's traceable only to Smith's Typewriters in the arcade below. And thousands of shoppers go by there daily. Easy for any one of the hundreds to type this on one of their machines. Like we did. Bye, Andi."

His face glowered in a white heat as he realised that what they said was true. He couldn't go to the police. What could he say to them? Besides, he had no clothes. For a moment he thought about sneaking out with the blanket tightly wrapped around him. But what if the police caught him? How could he explain?

He pulled open the door and walked toward the counter. Outside, Castlereagh Street was ablaze with lights. It was Saturday night. He couldn't take the risk. Musing, he picked up the paper bag that held the hamburger and took a bite of the meat-filled roll. Hmmm. Still warm. And good. He felt starved.

His teeth tearing at the roll and meat as if he had not eaten for weeks, he gazed about the shop. Racks and racks of clothes gazed back at him. But not a male garment in sight. Maybe he could find a blouse and suit jacket that fitted him. Some slacks? Where were the larger sizes?

If passersby had pressed their noses to the window, they might have noticed in the dark recesses of the shop a man, tears of fury and humiliation welling in his eyes, trying first this jacket, then that, up against his white torso for size. Later, they'd have seen him not at all. Exhausted, finding nothing to fit him, Mr Andreoni had retired to his office chair, resigned to waiting out Saturday night, Sunday, and the interminable hours lying between him and the first postal delivery on Monday.

He thought not once of his cat, Trixi, who indeed thought little of him as she lapped up the saucer of cream Mercy had brought by for her, then later cleaned her paws in smug contentment after feasting on a large piece of fresh fish, it, too, courtesy of Mercy Adamson.

"Andreoni's Fashion Boutique doesn't seem to be doing so well since you left, Tania," said one of the assistants at her new place of employment, just along the arcade, The Persimmon.

"Mmmm. Seems I got out just at the right time," responded Tania Siddons, bustling over to assist a customer whose head was poking out between the curtains of a dressingroom, obviously looking for help.

In the front of the shop, Mercy was rearranging the models in the widow. She had found her forte in window dressing and advertising. As she adjusted the "new season's fashions", and with an artistic eye decided on the right place for each of the large cardboard signs she had designed, she glanced down toward Andreoni's. Mr Andreoni lurched into view. He looked as if he had just had a horrifying experience. His head was clutched in his hands, and he was shaking it from side to side.

There he had been, walking down King Street towards Castlereagh and Centrepoint, when Mr Andreoni saw Mrs Peterson coming towards him. Fine figure of a woman, he thought as they drew closer. And he certainly knew her figure. A regular customer, Mrs Peterson. Regularly in his shop. Regularly in his dressing rooms.

Why, she was wearing that green suit she'd bought just the other day. He had seen her trying it on. (Wouldn't let those women get the better of him. He had chipped out one of the plaster of paris plugs he had inserted that horrible day when– It *was* only one. One little peephole. A man couldn't be blamed.)

Suddenly, he saw Mrs Peterson cross the street. She had one hand in her pocket. And she was snubbing him. Snubbing *him*. Furiously, he strode toward the shop. Then his steps began to falter. His knees sagged. This couldn't go on. All his regulars – they were deserting him. Soon, he'd be left with a shop full of clothes, one mean little peephole, and no customers. It wasn't right. It just wasn't right! Oh. If only he could get back at that Tania and Mercy and Dacey. How he rued the day he took them on. It was all their fault.

As Mrs Peterson walked swiftly away, her hand fingered the pocket in the right hand side of the jacket she wore, closing around a piece of paper screwed into a ball. She remembered vividly taking home the suit in one of the large brown and gold plastic bags from Mr Andreoni's shop. "Andreoni's Fashion Boutique" read the words along one side of the bag. "London, Paris, Sydney," read the other.

In haste to show her daughter, Rose, she had pulled the suit sharply out from the tissue paper that lay between the folds of material.

"What's this, Mum?" Rose had picked up what looked like an advertising flyer which lay half in, half out, of the plastic bag.

"Oh, just some advertisement. Some new idea of Andreoni's...Put it into every bag, I expect, so customers read it when they get home." She was busy concentrating on fitting the green skirt over her hips.

"No, Mum, you read it." Rose held it up. spreading it against her chest so her mother could see the words clearly printed in black and red on a white background:

"Mr Andreoni is a sexual harasser and a Peeping Tom. Stamp out sexual harassment and peeping."

"What on earth...Good heavens, Rose, do you think it's true?"

"Well, Mum, that's what it says. D'you think it's a case of self-advertisement – or did someone else put it in the bag?"

"But – but he served me himself. It – it must have already been in there..."

Their eyes met.

Walking along King Street, Mrs Peterson remembered the message:

"Mr Andreoni is a sexual harasser..."

As she thrust her hand into her pocket, wondering whether she should greet Mr Andreoni in the ordinary way, or do her best to avoid him, she touched a piece of paper. What? she thought. She hadn't noticed it previously. But it must have been there when she bought the suit. She had put nothing in the pockets.

Trembling slightly, her fingers drew out a single page and unfolded it. She held it in front of her whilst she paused for a moment: "Mr Andreoni is a sexual harasser and a Peeping Tom," she read, the red and black letters standing out on the white background:

"Stamp out sexual harassment and peeping."

Heels clattering on the footpath, her feet carried her across the pavement and out of the range of Mr Andreoni. How many others? she thought. Hundreds? Tens of hundreds? She held her chin high as she swept across the street.

Dacey, Tania and Mercy sat around a table at the Medieval Coffee Shop, nibbling raisin toast between sips of cappuccino. "Money's just come through," said Dacey. "Good old Great Aunt Olive. She recognised the need for independence in a woman."

"Mmmm," nodded Tania and Mercy together. "We've got some news too."

Dacey looked up. "Don't tell me – the loan's come through?"

"Women's Trust," said Tania. "We got the letter yesterday. They're prepared to lend $70,000 at 10%."

"Well, girls, what with your $70,000 and my $35,000, we've enough to buy our own business, a three woman partnership. Two designers, a window-dresser-cum-public-relations-lady. And three entrepreneurial sales women. Any businesses around, going cheap?" asked Dacey, raising her eyebrows at the others.

"Hear tell there's a shop down the arcade – stock going very cheap. Little or no goodwill to be sold," said Mercy. "I think if we get our agent to put in a bid, we'll be home and hosed as they say in the suburbs."

"And easy enough to change the name," chipped in Tania. "After all, need to get rid of only one word. 'D.M.T. Fashion Boutique' has a certain ring to it, doesn't it?"

Courier for the Underground

THE WHITE VAN with dark blue lettering down one side trundled slowly down the road, stopping first at the red brick on the corner then, three doors along, at a house which could hardly be seen from the street. Trees filled the garden, leafy green boughs hanging over the ivy clad fence and into the grassy nature strip.

A few minutes, then the white van was on its way, driving more quickly this time, and coming to a halt eight or ten houses up the road. Five minutes later, it was off again, turning left into Murchison Street and leaving Brentwood Road behind. The van came to a jerking stop at the house with the brown shutters five along from the intersection of Murchison Street and Dowel Circuit. Shortly after, it started up and turned into Dowel Circuit, coming to a halt once or twice, then driving off toward Charnwood.

Three hours later, back at Belconnen, the van stopped. Jumping down from the cab, the driver walked around, whistling, to the rear doors. Taking a deep breath, he turned the handle, pulling the right hand door towards him. Leaning in, he grabbed up several large white cannisters, holding them outwards, away from his body.

Soaked in some special solution and, anyway, packed in airtight, odourless containers, the nappies nonetheless exuded an aura of – Grimacing, he started off down the path toward the plain brick building. "Happy Nappy Inc." read the sign in large neon letters. "Happy Nappy Inc." also appeared on a plaque to the left of the front door. Walking in, the van driver waved a cheery hello to Joe, who was standing by the enquiry counter, as always, chatting up Doreen, the receptionist-cum-secretary-cum-telephonist. Then it was down the corridor, to two large iron doors, which swung apart as he approached.

"G'day, how many you got there?" asked the man who sat just inside. "How's it going out there in happy nappy land?" "No problems," responded Darryn, the driver. "They're really having a ball out there, I can tell you. Must be the Canberra diet. Those babies sure use up the nappies, mate." Expertly, with a turn of the arm born of long experience, Darryn threw the cannisters in a curving arc, right into one of the large wire baskets which stood on wheels, over at the side, near the wall. "And there's more where those came from," he said, jerking his head back in the direction of the front of the building, the road, and the van. "Back shortly, Frank."

Canberra was a great place for any business, so long as it was connected with home-and-garden. And home-and-garden mostly included, in Canberra, babies-in-the-garden, until they turned into tots-in-childcare, then kiddies-down-the-road-at-school, to be joined by more babies-in-the-garden, whether in the one household or the house next door. Some suburbs – Anslie, Turner, Barton – held aging populations. The schools and colleges were being closed down, to the howls of the young middle-aged who had grown up in the great days of the demonstrations against Vietnam, and knew what activism was all about. In some households, the demonstrations were all the more heartfelt, as they embarked on second marriages and second families, or the women who had taken a career path, now forty or forty three, decided to heed the biological clock. And the newer suburbs – Richardson, Charnwood, Theodore, Calwell – kept shooting up, spawning young couples who in turn spawned families, so that the houses swelled with the sound of babies crying for the 4.00 AM feed, and the 6.00 AM feed, and because they were teething. And in the middle of the day, out came the harried mothers, pushing the prams with strings of rattles in the shape of rabbits and ducks slung across from one side to the other. The women made quick visits to the local shops, mostly, and less often to the local parks dotted around.

Canberra had its less financially advantaged suburbs, too. The housing complex at Melba, and the inner suburbs of the Causeway, stranding women on welfare, sole parents with two or three children, isolated in the midst of middle-class affluence, public service jobs and university degrees. Anxiously, they juggled with the rent and the food and shoes for the kids, the bottles and formula, the nappies and rusks, all on $150.80 per week, plus $27.40 for each child under 13 years of age, or $39.95 for each child between 13 and 15 years, and a $2.60 pharmaceutical allowance. Oh, and maybe $36.20 rent assistance (maximum), together with $41.40 family allowance for two children.

When they could, they placed the children in childcare, then went out into the job market, taking what they could get. Some of them got Happy Nappy Inc. There, amongst the nappy wash, it was almost an extension of home. But there, at least, washing nappies was paid.

And into all this, on his regular round five days a week, came Darryn, the Happy Nappy Inc. driver, collecting the dirties, delivering the fresh packages containing pristine squares of brushed cotton. Meryl Sanderson, of the red brick on the corner in Brentwood Road, looked forward to his arrival on Mondays and Thursdays. It was not only that she could then relieve the overflowing containers in the laundry of their bowel-filled bundles in exchange for the white packages stamped with the familiar blue Happy Nappy Inc. logo, the content of which was, by that time, vital for the seemingly never ending output of newly arrived Baby Florence. Nor was it that she longed for the sight of Darryn himself, even though he was the only adult she saw, apart from the people at the shop, through the long lonely hours of the day. Rather, there were the messages.

She made the first discovery on a Monday back in June. It was particularly cold and wet, one of those Canberra days when the wind blows fiercely, making it impossible to go outside. Even the loaf of bread she was hungering for, longing to make into toast with a liberal scraping of butter and honey, couldn't get her out, down the road. Darryn appeared on the red asphalt doorstep at 12.01 PM, with no explanation for being two hours behind his usual schedule, just grabbing the plastic bundle, full of once-damp smells, from her, thrusting his clinical-looking package into her arms in exchange. Then he was off, speeding a little today in the small white van, up to the house with the trees, third in the street, then on again, and into Murchison Street and around, well out of sight of Brentwood Road, the red brick, and Meryl. She turned and sighed, slowly walking back into the kitchen where she sat for a moment, looking at the bundle half in gratitude, half horror at the realisation of the long weeks and months stretching out in front of her, weeks and months of nappies. But at least there were no weeks and months of scraping the little, rich-ochre deposits into the water at the bottom of the porcelain lavatory bowl, then soaking the once white squares in the laundry sink, now. Darryn and Happy Nappy Inc. would be back on her doorstep twice weekly to take the containers away, containers full of nappies which she was no longer obliged to wash. Happy Nappy Inc. did it all.

No point in just sitting here, she thought, and tugged at the binding around the package. She lifted out the nappies, patting them gently as she placed them, one by one, on top of each other on the kitchen table. And then she saw it. There, between two of the firmly folded white squares, a crisp white envelope addressed "To the Woman of the House". The bill? It had never been presented this way before, between the nappies. Always, it came by hand, Darryn's hand, on the Thursdays. Thursday was payday in Canberra, a public service habit that brushed off on private enterprise as well, however small or large the business. Thursday and payday were synonymous in Canberra. An advertisement? She almost threw it, unopened, in the bin. Then her hand paused as she read the message swiftly, once more: "To the Woman of the House".

Even in Canberra, no one advertised in this way. The Australian Bureau of Statistics had only just stopped addressing its surveys and the census to the "man of the house" in the presumption that "head of household" meant "man". Though Canberrans prided themselves on their greater progressiveness than the rest of the country, old attitudes died hard, even here.

She tore at the envelope, inserting her index finger under the long flap at the back. Out came the single sheet of paper. Unfolding it, she read: "Women Rise Up. You have nothing to lose but your chains!"

On that same Monday, further along Darryn's Happy Nappy Inc. route, five doors down from the intersection of Murchison Street and Dowel Circuit, in the house with the brown shutters, Cecily Roseneath had yet to discover her envelope. She had been pacing the floor when Darryn at last pressed the bell, just below the hunting lamp that was affixed on the creamy white wall, contrasted against the shutters. The epitome of good taste, Cecily thought. Well, she had thought in the days she had time to think about such things. But the life of the mother-at-home had rather put a stop to all that. Samantha Roseneath was a happy baby. But rather too happy, thought Cecily, a little grimly, sometimes. It was always happy babies who gurgled and drank and ate, contentedly centring all their energy on their bodily habits. Eat and excrete was the style of the happy baby, Cecily Roseneath had learned in the seven months of Sam's delighted existence. And it meant that two deliveries a week were really not enough. Two lots of freshly laundered nappies hardly sufficient to take her through the long week. Long weeks of feeding and washing and wiping and changing and powdering. And at times lavishly spreading what seemed to be mountains of vaseline on the firm, round, pink bottom of Sam.

The weekend had been a particularly happy time for Samantha, the happy baby. But today, she was actually squawking in her cot, her little legs circling in bicycle motions, her fist clenched hard up against her open mouth, her eyes screwed tightly closed, all her energy directed at the discomfort of lying, humiliatedly naked from the waist down, on a blanket so obviously covering a rubber mattress protector. "It's all very well," she seemed to be shouting through the squawls. "I know I can't control my bodily functions yet, mother. But at least you could cover it up with the usual clean, white square, in its 'v', neatly folded, not leave me like this, mother."

Darryn almost fell backwards, into the flowerbed full of its rich brown-red soil, as Cecily grabbed the proffered package with great force. With not a single clean nappy left, matters in the Roseneath household had reached a level of seriousness not previously matched.

Just as he recovered his balance, Darryn found himself pushed against once more, this time the large, plastic, nappy-filled canister slapping against his shins and knees and thighs. Cecily had made more than a fair exchange.

"Hey, hold on," he exclaimed. But the door had already closed. Behind it, the package was torn apart, its sweet smelling contents scattered over the hall carpet. Samantha gave one last, frantic blast, then purred contentedly as Cecily, with a skill born of long practice, swiftly and efficiently secured the nappy between the baby's legs and around her waist.

Sitting back on her heels in the hall, Cecily Roseneath gathered up the white squares. And it was then she saw the envelope, addressed in clear letters: "To the Woman of the House". Can't mean anyone but me, she mused, the evidence of it sleeping, for now, in the cot up the passage.

Nappies under one arm, she went into the kitchen, poured a cup of coffee from the pot she kept perking on the bench next to the sink, and sat down to read. "Women Rise Up. You have nothing to lose but your chains!" Like Meryl Sanderson's missive, it bore the sign of a clenched fist, broken chain dangling from the hand, down to the wrist. The fist was superimposed upon the symbol of a sturdy cross supporting a firmly rounded circle. Under the symbol were written the words: "Women Supporting Women Collective."

For Susan Standen, in the house with the trees, three down from Meryl Sanderson, that Monday in June had brought the same message: "Women, Rise Up…" As it had for Dana Trigg and Jennifer Howell, living along Dowel Circuit. And the messages hadn't stopped. Every Monday, the women on Darryn's Happy Nappy Inc. route waited eagerly for their delivery. Every Monday, there was something new. Quotations from Elizabeth Cady Stanton and Susan B. Anthony accompanied the nappies:

"The labor of women in the house, certainly, enables men to produce more wealth than they otherwise could; and in this way women are economic factors in society. But so are horses."

"...we shall never become an immense power in the world until we concentrate all our money and editorial forces upon one great national daily newspaper, so we can sauce back our opponents every day in the year..."

These were intermingled with the words of Margaret Fuller and Elizabeth Janeway:

"A home is no home unless it contains food and fire for the mind as well as for the body."

"Power is the ability not to have to please."

Sometimes longer extracts appeared, some from home-grown women activists. Germaine Greer featured several times. Marilyn Waring spoke out on economics. Dale Spender was a favourite. Meryl had particularly liked a quotation from *Women of Ideas:*

"...for centuries women have been challenging men...For centuries women have been claiming that the world and men look very different from the perspective of women..."

She had read it out loud to Florence, lying sleeping quietly in her crib at four months. Later, when Florence was awake and chirping merrily, the two had gone out into the Canberra late afternoon sunlight and Meryl had ordered a copy of the book through Robertson's, the newsagent in the local shopping centre. The woman behind the counter had looked interested. "I've read something about that book, I think. Wasn't she in Canberra recently? I think I heard her interviewed on that morning programme on the ABC." Meryl was disappointed. Until the message brought through Happy Nappy Inc. and the cheerful services of Darryn, she hadn't known of Dale Spender's existence, much less about her books or her visit to Canberra. Hadn't heard her on the radio. Still, she knew now. And she was getting the book. "I might get a copy in for myself as well," said the saleswoman. "I can always give it to my daughter if I can't be bothered with it."

Dana Trigg liked a piece from Anne Summers' *Damned Whores and God's Police*. She had tried reading it out to her husband Robert, but he hadn't been listening, too absorbed behind the flapping pages of the *Canberra Times*. She went into the bedroom and read it out loud, to herself, lying on the bed with one arm behind her head, thinking.

As the weeks and months went by, Susan Standen and Meryl Sanderson discovered their tastes in "best bits" were similar. They and Dana Trigg and Jennifer Howell often had fast and furious debates about what Germaine Greer and Dale Spender and Kate Millett and Gloria Steinem and Betty Friedan had said. Cecily Roseneath usually sat, taking it all in, putting in a comment now and then. When she did, they all paused, listening. They had grown to know of her silences and that, when she spoke, they should not miss what she said.

This was all new. They had never known each other before the first missive arrived amongst the nappies washed so fluffily by Happy Nappy Inc. Meryl had brought all that about. With the help of Darryn, certainly. But she prided herself on her initiative, nonetheless.

One Thursday, when the messages first started coming, Meryl had decided that she would send a message back to Happy Nappy Inc., and discover who else was receiving the messages she got through Darryn. She realised she was waiting eagerly, every week, for Monday to come around, to see what the next message would be. The second Monday, she had wondered if there would be any message at all. Maybe it was a one-off, just someone fooling around to no purpose. But no. That was the week she received the message:

"There are hazards in anything one does, but there are greater hazards in doing nothing."

That was the British politician, Social Democrat Shirley Williams.

"Yes," thought Meryl, catching herself nodding in agreement. From then on, she quickly lost any apprehension that the envelope would not be there with the next Monday nappy delivery. She began to wonder who it was sending the messages. A woman, it went without saying. Maybe more than one?

That Thursday, she went to Belconnen early, taking the bus and braving the pram problem. The bookshop would surely have something in stock with a suitable extract. And if it didn't have a photocopying machine, the chemist probably would.

Running her hand quickly along the shelves, Meryl found a copy of *The Feminist Dictionary*. Cheris Kramarae and Paula Treichler, she read. She chose a short extract for this first message, worried that it might not get to the right person. What system did they have at Happy Nappy Inc. for sorting out nappies from the various households, Meryl wondered. There was no assurance that her nappies would necessarily get to the woman who every week, and on odd occasions twice a week (some messages were now coming on Thursday, too), concealed an envelope addressed "To the Woman of the House". They might get to her eventually, though they could be sorted by someone else first. Meryl was ready to take the chance. After all, the woman at Happy Nappy Inc. had the courage to send out messages, messages some would see as of a highly questionable kind (subversive, even) to a woman of whom she knew nothing, out here in the heartland of suburban Canberra. It could have caused a terrible stink. The woman could have lost her job.

"Inertia, Law of: Bodies in power tend to stay in power, unless external forces disturb them."

That was perfect for the first try-out, thought Meryl. She bought some white envelopes, pondering on how she might address them. She had decided that if this one got through without any fuss, there would be more. It would be "them".

She felt a thrill of pleasure as she put twenty cents into the machine and took up the copy as it spat out the end. Subversion in the household being met with subversion in the laundry. It had all sorts of possibilities.

Hurrying back to Brentwood Road, just in time to catch Darryn on his round, Meryl decided she would find whomever else was in receipt of the messages. Little reason to believe she was the only one. Why choose her bundle of nappies over anyone else's?

Darryn came tootling up to the house, parking the white van carefully at the side of the road, getting out, opening the back doors and taking his time about selecting her package. Slow, for once (just because she was eagerly waiting, the white-sheathed bundle in her hand, a white envelope, covered in a plastic bag from the market, hidden between the baby-battered pieces of warm cotton), Meryl grumbled to herself.

At last, he was on the front step. They exchanged bundles. Meryl went straight back into the house, concerned not to allow him to believe there was anything different today. But of course there was. And it was not only that she, in turn, had turned him into a courier service. It was that she had decided to follow him on his round. To find out about the others.

Florence was already asleep, her dummy close by her pert pink mouth. Meryl took the chance. Usually, once asleep that was it for Florence for a few good hours, and the jaunt out to Belconnen had no doubt tired her even more than usual. Out went Meryl, walking close to the leafy verges, trying to keep out of the range of the rear vision mirror of the Happy Nappy Inc. van.

The van had stopped at the house with the trees, three further along Brentwood Road. She saw Darryn start up again, then come to a halt at the house eight along. Then it was around to Murchison Street and Dowel Circuit, five down from the intersection, the house with the brown shutters. Meryl wrote the numbers down on a piece of paper she had brought with her, watching as she did so the van stopping at two other houses in Dowel Circuit. That was enough. At least for today. She walked back along the street, deciding to try the house closest to hers, first.

They had grown into a friendly group. They met over lunch and coffee and morning tea, arguing, discussing, debating. At the centre of the arguments, the discussions, the debates were the quotations, and the books from which they came. Just as Meryl Sanderson had gone to the newsagent to order Dale Spender's book early on, she discovered Susan Standen, Dana Trigg, Cecily Roseneath and Jennifer Howell had done the same, ordering Robin Morgan's books, along with whatever Simone de Beauvoir and Germaine Greer had published. And new names kept cropping up through the bundles of nappies. Old, now familiar, names reappeared. Betty Friedan's book, *The Feminine Mystique*, had been hard to get at first. It was Dana Trigg who initially ordered it, to be told it was out of stock – or even, perhaps, out of print. But shortly after, it must have been (before they met one another), Jennifer Howell went in and ordered it too.

Lurline Symons, whom they came to know as the assistant at the newsagent's, told her of the huge interest women in the neighbourhood had shown in the book. Lurline had had no less than seven orders for it already, and all in the space of a few days. She would hurry the distributors along. It had been out of stock, she told Jennifer, but the Sydney arm of the publishers had told her the demand had got the British distributors back on the job. Now there were stocks on the way, so they said.

"I'll get right on to that lot," she said. "If it's not here by Friday I'll – I'll drive up to Sydney myself. If we can't get them moving what with all this interest here in Canberra, I don't know what will," she added, nodding determinedly. "My daughter's asking for it too."

Their orders poured in. Robert Trigg was still grunting behind the *Canberra Times*, or concentrating on whatever was on television, when Dana tried to read bits of the books to him. He didn't seem to realise the housekeeping money was going on establishing a good library for Dana and his daughter Tulip. Still, thought Dana, shrugging her shoulders. I'm doing my best to share it with him. Not my fault he's a literary philistine. Nor did Colin Sanderson know what a few left over dollars bought. Meryl's housekeeping had deteriorated to a "lick and a promise" in between reading whatever Lurline Symons had got in that week.

"But," she reflected. "It still looks presentable. Beds made. Dishes done. Not so much vacuuming. But nothing wrong with a bit of dust, anyway." She read on. The group talked on.

They began sending books through Darryn of Happy Nappy Inc. He, abiding by his routine, carried out his deliveries and collections, unaware of his new and developing role. They, careful, always, to wrap the books tightly in plastic so that the covers and pages would not get damp, or something worse, packaged with the goods destined for the laundry. Often, now, discussion lingered on their mysterious benefactor at Happy Nappy Inc. Who was she? Or they. Jennifer and Dana and Cecily and Meryl and Susan bought the latest books, ordering them through Lurline, hoping they weren't duplicating anything their benefactor already had.

Sometimes, now, when they were talking, Colin Sanderson might come into the kitchen, as if to say this is my kitchen, looking around as if to ask why they were there, what right had they, taking up his kitchen with all this feminist talk. But they didn't even glance at him. Paid him no attention. Meryl didn't leap up, get him a cup of coffee, or tea, or even hand him the plate piled high with biscuits they seemed always to have. Coffee creams. Or chocolate Tim Tams. Or Venetians. Or even "home baked cookies", biscuits filled with large pieces of apricot, or fat raisins and chunky bits of orange rind, from the bakehouse over at Belconnen. Always very expensive, rich looking biscuits. Truth to tell, Meryl didn't even notice he was there. And it was the same for Michael Standen, when they sat, talking, talking, in what he had until now thought of as *his* loungeroom. Susan just went on talking. They all did. And Paul Howell began to come home at odd hours, to find them around the diningroom table. But Jennifer just kept talking. Robert Trigg gave up reading the *Canberra Times*. He would turn off the television set when they were meeting at the red brick house on the corner of Brentwood Road, doing his utmost to draw attention to himself. But Meryl and Susan and Dana and Jennifer just talked on, whilst Cecily sat concentrating, then chipping in. They had nothing to lose.

"WOMEN, RISE UP. You have nothing to lose but your chains." The sign flashed on to television screens throughout the Canberra suburbs, and at Parliament House and in the offices where public servants worked back, clocking up the overtime. It led the six o'clock news on Channel 7. Jennifer Howell saw it as she tidied up the lounge-room after putting Timothy to bed. Dana Trigg noticed the placard with its familiar message as she folded the *Canberra Times*. Her hand paused as she stood mesmerised by what was happening on the screen.

"HAPPY NAPPY INC. EXPLOITS THE WORKERS!" The cameras picked out placards held high by a group of women who were circulating in front of a large white building. Atop the white bricks, the neon sign read in bold white and blue letters: "Happy Nappy Inc."

Suddenly, regaining herself, Dana ran to the telephone. Meryl Sanderson answered excitedly. "You saw it too," she exclaimed. "We'd better get on to the others to make sure they're tuned in. Let's see if it's on SBS and the ABC as well, then we'd better get back to each other. We'd better do something."

"We've put up with under award conditions for long enough from Happy Nappy," said the tall woman holding one end of a "WOMEN, RISE UP..." banner. "We're doing a good day's work, and we demand a good day's pay."

"And healthy conditions." The camera shot across to the other end of the banner, where a woman in a white uniform glared firmly at its lens. "We're sick of working with water sloshing around our feet, and no proper break for lunch. Happy Nappy thinks we don't know our rights, and that we're not entitled to them, anyway. We're staying out until they agree to proper conditions and award rates."

"Yayyy!" chorused the five or six women standing around her, their placards waving in unison. "Happy Nappy exploits the workers. Happy Nappy exploits the workers." The chant rose up, beyond the cameras and microphones, swirling around the large white and blue neon letters. "Women, rise up..." The words faded into background noise as a man walked towards the camera, his face beaming handsomely, yet with a seriousness befitting the storyline, as he held the microphone at just the right height, in the middle of his be-suited chest. His voice, at the appropriate pitch, the tones mellow yet engaged, asked of the Canberra viewers:

"How long will the women stay out? How long before the Mums of Canberra demand a better deal for their nappies? Will the strike break when the Mums descend on Happy Nappy demanding the workers return to the job of washing *their* babies' nappies? This is Martin De Vries reporting on-site from the picket line at Happy Nappy Inc., the sole nappy wash business in Canberra."

The picture faded, the cameras refocusing in the studio, where a serious looking person sitting at a desk began the next story.

Susan Standen dashed to the phone. "Meryl, we've got to do something. It's true what he's saying. We n-e-e-d Happy Nappy. But Vera Swindon says they're exploited. What're we going to do?"

Vera Swindon seemed to be the spokeswoman. She had done most of the talking to the cameras and journalists milling around the Happy Nappy work-site. Now strike-site. While Susan was talking to Meryl, Jennifer and Cecily were echoing their words, and Dana, almost hopping from one foot to the other, anxious to telephone any one of them, was caught by Robert reading some item to her from the newspaper. She dashed, to find Meryl's line engaged. Guessing what was happening, she put her head in the lounge room door. "I'm just running up the street for a moment, Robert. The dinner's in the oven. You go ahead and start. I'll be back soon." Without waiting for a reply, she was out and into Dowel Circuit. As she swept up the steps of the Howell household, she saw Meryl rushing toward her along the street. Jennifer opened the door to welcome them both. Behind them, Cecily Roseneath and Susan Standen appeared, joining them in the kitchen.

"Okay, women. It's war," declared Meryl. "Our nappies just have to be washed. There's no two ways about it. *And* they have to be washed under decent conditions. We're paying enough, for heavens sake. What's happening to all the profits, that's what I want to know."

"Darryn collected twenty from me on Monday, and I'm down to my last three," wailed Dana. "Tulip will be soooo angry without her 'whiter than whites'. How could Happy Nappy *do* this to us?"

"Well," declared Cecily firmly. "Sam's just about out, too. This can't go on. I vote we take a strong stand. Happy Nappy has just got to get back into production. That laundry has to start working. Properly." Four heads nodded in agreement. In their respective homes, five husbands sat down to the meal each had taken from the oven, and began their solitary eating.

Robert Trigg turned on the television set. He had come home to a silent house, and was still bemused. There was a note sitting on the top of workbench in the kitchen, telling him there was chicken in the freezer which had only to be taken out and placed on the plate in the microwave.

"Only!" he exclaimed to himself, annoyed. What was going on here?

And vegetables (from the freezer) could be done in the same way. He had walked outside, just to clear his head. Never before had he come home not to find cooking smells wafting through the house, the table laid, ready for the evening meal, the television on so that all he had to do was walk in, dump his brief case, pull off his shoes, then sit down to the news.

Outside, the dissonance was even greater. There on the wind-back washing line flapped rows and rows of white squares. Nappies. But he didn't know Dana *had* so many nappies. He knew babies used lots of the things, but surely Tulip alone couldn't fill four lines, stretching from the trellis near the barbecue to the garage. And why were they being washed at home, anyway. Didn't Dana use that nappy service? Oh, yes – Happy Nappy Inc. – and the strike.

The six o'clock news was just beginning. The strike at Happy Nappy led it once more. Chanting began to make itself heard, throbbing over the picture of placards waving, and a large banner stretching from one side of the screen to the other: "WOMEN, RISE UP..."

"What do we want?"

"Award wages."

"When do we want them?"

"Now!"

"What do we want?"

"Decent conditions."

"When do we want 'em?"

"Now!"

Martin de Vries, his smoothly handsome face smiling, but serious, concerned, looking deep into the lens, began:

"Here again at Happy Nappy Inc., the strike is continuing. But the numbers of demonstrators has swelled. It seems as if something important is happening here. This is the seventh day. It's the longest strike Canberra has ever seen, at least in recent times."

The camera focused on two women holding one end of the banner. "Well," thought Robert. "What d'you expect. Don't those women always look as if what they need is a good..." Suddenly, he looked more closely at the picture filling the screen. One of the women looked decidedly familiar. Wasn't it Meryl Sanderson from around the corner? Poor Col. What would he think about his wife involved in a get up like this. Was it good old Col's wife? He'd seen her around here often enough lately, as it was. All the coffee drinking and chattering that had been going on in this household. His brow wrinkled with concentration.

As always happens with the "four second clip" on television, and the fear of boring viewers with "talking heads", the picture changed. Just as Robert Trigg had almost assured himself that yes, it was Meryl Sanderson, Martin de Vries thrust the microphone under the chin of another woman, who was standing in a group, holding a placard reading "WOMEN UNITE". Robert's heart stopped. That face was all too familiar. It was Dana. Dana. And she had Tulip perched under her arm. "What the hell..."

"Dana Trigg," Martin de Vries mellow tones began. "You've joined the strikers here, outside Happy Nappy Inc., to fight for better wages and conditions." "Yes," responded Dana, looking straight into the camera, into the eyes of Robert, her husband, who was sitting, collapsed against the arm of the lounge, gasping. "We have joined the workers to fight in unity for their rights, for the rights of women workers." "Yaayyy! Women. Unite," came the chanting sounds from the background.

Vera Swindon, now a face well known to the Canberra television audience, stood by Dana's side. Then, to her left, Robert saw the rest of the bunch he had grown used to seeing sitting around in his kitchen. And there seemed to be more. There were hoards of women. He got up slowly, dragging himself toward the phone. As he reached out, it rang. "Bob, Bob, is that you?" a hoarse voice emitted from the ear piece. It was Colin Sanderson. "We're all over at Paul's. Get over here. This is serious." When Robert Trigg walked in, they were hunched around the television set, watching the SBS news and waiting to see it all again on the ABC newsbroadcast at 7.00 PM. Like Robert, they were trying to tell themselves it wasn't true. It wasn't their wives down at Happy Nappy Inc., carrying on with placards and banners and other women, their children caught up in this – this – demonstration. Maybe the pictures on the ABC would tell a different story.

They had commandeered Darryn's van early on. Cecily drove it on the usual round, which was easy to chart from the address labels that were attached to each plastic bundle as it was brought into the laundry. Vera Swindon and her colleagues had a good recall for all the names, all the addresses. They sat up late one night, completing the list and making plans. They ran rosters on a daily basis. Women who came from Anslie and Forrest, Griffith and Barton, Lyneham and Turner, joined up, too. The messages had got through to them as they washed and dusted their babies' bottoms, packed and unpacked the nappies.

Nappies were washed and returned, even whiter than white, even more promptly than before. Washing machines in the houses in Brentwood Road and Murchison Street and Dowel Crescent churned through the days. Teams of women hung out the nappies, then folded and packed them. Inserting new messages of hope. And the bills went out, with a request that payment be made direct to the driver. Receipts would be issued immediately. The strike fund filled and overflowed. Happy Nappy's resources dwindled.

The white van shot briskly up the street, came to a firm halt, and the driver leapt out. Doreen, smart in a navy blue suit, greeted the driver at the main entrance, as usual, with a friendly smile. "Just go on down," she said. "They're getting through them by the dozen down there. Shouting out for more work, as I hear it." Efficiently, she noted the names and numbers of nappies in the computer which now sat primly on a shiny new desk just inside the glassy reception area. Plants lined up greenly along the corridor.

"Got my ten o'clock load here," said the driver to the woman standing at the head of the row of churning, shining washing machines that glinted in the clean air, the overhead lights. "Thanks, Cecily." Susan Standen smiled. She glanced down the line, toward Dana Trigg, who was enthusiastically bundling nappies into the line of machines. Over in the next area of the large space, Jennifer Howell was transferring nappies into the driers. Meryl Sanderson was working in the office, alongside Trudy Martenson, one of the residents of the Melba flats. Vera Swindon was out at a local advertising agency, making a series of new advertisements for Happy Nappy Inc. Collectively, they had decided to project a new image, the image of positive and important work going on at Happy Nappy. Work that kept the world going around. Nappies washed on time, with real energy, hanging out for drying in the warm sun in summer, and in the days when Canberra's winters allowed natural drying. Even when dried in the machines, the nappies were later hung out in a drying room, to be wafted with a special fanning mechanism installed by the new owners of Happy Nappy Inc.

Oh. And the name had been changed. Now it was registered, the shares increasing in value, the work load increased, the wages over-award, the conditions splendid. The sign makers hadn't batted an eyelid at the request. "Happy Nappy Collective Inc." read the neon sign in white and blue over the large white building. And on the left hand side, the motto appeared, as it appeared on the letterhead, now. "Women. Rise."

Bad Cooking

"JUDY! JU-DY! WHAT is this? Ju-dy!"

Judy Melton came hurrying from the kitchen, carrying in both hands a large bowl of steaming vegetables. Carefully, she set it down on a cork placemat, then looked up at Roger, whose face was raging. He pounded the table.

"How often do I have to say it, Judy. This food just isn't fit to eat. What's it supposed to be?"

"It's pork chops, as you like them, Roger, and I've added a new sauce of..."

Before she could finish, he was pounding the table again. She knew what was coming. She had heard it all so often before. Whatever she did, it wasn't good enough.

"Decent food. That's what I want. Something I can eat. Anything that can survive your cooking, woman. What's a man to do if he can't eat?"

A few more imprecations, a glaring look, then the shouting and pounding stopped. Roger stared down at his plate, ignoring her as she sat opposite, picking at the vegetables she had added to the untouched chop in front of her. With his left hand he propelled a large piece of meat towards his mouth, whilst with his right he thrust a large serving spoon into the hot bowl on the cork mat, scooping-up carrots and potatoes in large chunks. After depositing them to one side of the sauce covered chops, back went the spoon for more. Peas and pumpkin made their way to his plate. He took up another large piece of meat on his fork. It disappeared into his mouth. The silence was filled with the methodical noises which regularly emitted from Roger's jaws, as they munched and chewed their way through this meal, just as they munched and chewed their way through every meal.

Ten or fifteen minutes passed, during which Roger filled his plate several times from the vegetable bowl, and took another serving of chops, smothered in their creamy smooth sauce, from the serving dish standing on his side of the table. He lunged at the wicker basket set to the left of his bread and butter plate. Taking a bread roll, Roger tore it in two and began soaking up the remaining sauce from his dinner plate. The plate wiped clean, he pushed it from him, across the table towards his wife.

"Well, what are you sitting there for woman. What's next, Judy? Surely that's not all?"

Silent, she rose, removing his empty plate and the remains of the main course lying on her own, and hurried back to the kitchen. Marguerite pudding for dessert. Would that satisfy him? She doubted it.

Every day of their married life seemed to have been the same. Roger loud and angry about her cooking skills – or lack of them. She trying valiantly to cook in the way he wanted. First, she had gone to his mother for tips. He had formed his tastes, at home, as a child and growing up. If she could emulate Mrs Roberson's cooking, that should do the trick, she thought. She had thought.

She began serving up shepherd's pie, Irish stew, ragout, and Welshrarebit, in between roast dinners (seven vegetables: carrots, pumpkin, potatoes, sweet potato, swede, brussels sprouts, peas or sometimes beans), grilled chops (pork or lamb) and steak (sometimes fillet, mostly rump). Faithfully, she followed Mrs Roberson's recipes and advice. But still Roger found fault.

Off she went to cookery classes at the Council for Adult Education. A course in "good Australian cooking" was advertised. "Back to the basics," it said. That, she thought, was definitely for her. Start with the basics, then move on to more adventurous meals. But the basics weren't good enough. Her basics weren't right. Roger's complaints grew louder.

She finished the CAE course, then repeated it twice. Still no satisfaction from Roger. Too embarrassed to return again, she graduated (or, at least, moved on) to classes at the local TAFE college, explaining her difficulties to the instructor.

"I just can't seem to get it right," she told Ms Perkins, chef, cook and cooking teacher extraordinaire (as she described herself). "Not to worry, my girl," exclaimed Ms Perkins in her hearty manner. "We'll get it right in a jiffy. There's no one yet that I haven't put on the right road to culinary perfection, and I'm not about to start with you. We're doing Italian for the next six weeks, French after that. I'm thinking about including Chinese as another six week course. Now, if you can't get the Italian down pat, I'm not Rhonda Perkins and you're not Judy Melton, okay." It was not a question. It was a given. Judy sighed with relief. Now, perhaps, she and Roger would be able to settle down to a peaceful married life. Oh, for calm and quiet, she almost groaned to herself.

But it was never enough. She went through basic cooking, Italian, French, Spanish, Chinese, Thai, Hawaiian. She tried American, thinking that surely it was impossible to ruin a plain hamburger or do damage to corned beef hash or a sloppy Joe. They went to dinner at friends' houses. Roger came home raving about the cooking. She consulted with the wives of Roger's friends, copying their recipes and even going so far as to borrow their cooking implements sometimes. Was the error in her kitchen rather than in her? It made no difference. "Judy, what is this? Ju-dy!"

Judy's cooking gained notoriety in the neighbourhood. Roger made jokes about it, not only to her, but across the fence to Simon Dance in the pauses between mowing their respective lawns. The motor mowers started up, ran for a time, then stopped. Then came the guffaws of laughter, and she knew Roger was entertaining Simon with yet another story about her cooking. One day she came upon them as they sat, having a smoko, on the front steps, the pages of the *Sydney Morning Herald* spread out between them at the racing section. Roger was holding up another part of the paper and reading an article to Simon, about a recall on food products that had just been ordered by the authorities.

"Salmonella recall on Euro-Prima products," he said loudly, nodding his head. "Hey, listen to this," he continued:

Salmonella bacteria may have contaminated more than 67,000 packets of dehydrated foods, some of which are on sale in New South Wales. The manufacturer Duo-decima has warned the public not to eat the three Euro-Prima brand products: one litre cream of mushroom packet soup and Dolza beef alpha and rice, and chicken alpha and rice.

The managing director of Duo-decima, Mr Justin Thompson, said the products had been recalled after the possibility of the salmonella contamination was discovered yesterday.

The salmonella scare was caused by the mistaken use in August of 24 cartons of mushrooms, a small number of which were contaminated by the bacteria, he said. The company had intended to return the mushrooms to the suppliers...

"Well, how about that, Simon," exclaimed Roger. "It goes on to say that people should return the goods to the retailer for a full refund...And wait for it, let me read this next bit," he said, laughing uproariously. Judy, who had crouched to pull at a few weeds growing in the garden, glanced over at him. Whatever was coming next, clearly it was a huge joke.

"'If the products are cooked strictly in accordance with the directions on the packet, they are perfectly safe,' Mr Thompson said. 'But the basic message is not to eat the products but return them to the retailer.' Ho, ho, ho. That much he knows," shouted Roger at the top of his voice. "Obviously this joker doesn't know my Judy. Why, Judy couldn't even cook them according to directions, never mind make them perfectly safe. Don't have to give her salmonella to put a man's stomach at risk. Har, har, har."

She saw Simon nodding, joining in the scoffing with Roger. Then Roger glanced over and saw her, standing by the corner of the house.

"Judy, Judy, did yah hear that? What we need around here is a food taster. Simon. Si. Will you be in it, mate? Do anything for your good mate Roger, wouldn't you," Roger yelled, clapping Simon on the back. "Now, Judy, don't go away. There's more to come."

Roger scrabbled amongst the papers lying at his side, dragging out the *Weekend Australian*, turning the pages until he came to the article he wanted. Standing and taking a theatrical pose, one hand on his heart, he read in a loud voice: "'Deadly bacteria discovered in three imported cheeses.' What about that, Si...Judy?" He glanced at them both, first at Simon, then at Judy, then guffawed loudly once more. "It goes on, wait for it." He held the page aloft, reading again in a booming voice:

> Government officials are investigating why inspection procedures in Australia, Italy, West Germany and France failed to detect a dangerous, life-threatening bacteria discovered in three cheeses tested for the *Australian*.
>
> Listeria monocytogenes, a little-understood pathogen which burst into world prominence only four years ago, was found during laboratory analyses of 53 soft cheeses bought by the *Australian* in New South Wales and Victoria.
>
> The suspect cheeses are manouri, imported from Greece, and milkana grunerpfeffer, imported from West Germany, and an imported blue.
>
> Listeria has been detected in Australian dairy factories five times in the past eighteen months, three in Victoria and two in New South Wales. While Australia has been spared an outbreak of the disease, epidemics of listeriosis in the United States and Europe have shown it to have a mortality rate of thirty per cent.
>
> "The dangerous strain, which has so far been isolated into thirteen types, is monocytogenes. 'Listeria is probably unavoidable in raw food. But if your hygiene is okay, that problem lessens,' Mr Sutherland said.

Judy looked at Roger's red, booming face. He hadn't finished yet, she was sure. And sure, there was more to come.

"Well, Judy, wadda yah reckon? No problems with hygiene around here, that's for certain. But the problem's not hygiene with you anyway, woman. The problem won't lessen, as they say, until you do some decent cooking." Roger's eyes met Simon's. They laughed uproariously again, the two of them. As usual, Judy said nothing. She just looked at them, then slowly turned to complete the weeding, pulling at the long pieces of green that were growing at the edges of the lawn and the flower beds.

One day, she discovered it. Driving around near Centennial Park and the showground, she stopped, as she often did, at a secondhand bookshop near a bus stop. She went in and began browsing, looking first at the bargain table, then moving on to the shelves. She ran her hand along the top shelf of the cookery section. Suddenly, she paused. This might be it.

A large book, it was pale brown – almost khaki. The spine carried the title *Cookery Around the World: The Cook's Encyclopædia*. She took it down and began turning the pages. The fly leaf almost fell out. It had partially come adrift from the spine. But the rest seemed in reasonably good order. Dated 1928, she noted. Miranda Davidson. Published in London. New Foliage Books. Printed in Czechoslovakia. Her eyes ran rapidly over the first words appearing under the heading "Introduction":

> Over the years, in the course of travelling, I have collected recipes from at home and abroad. My friends, too, have contributed to my collection. The variety of 'cooking abroad', its very simplicity, and its sheer perfection, cried out for an audience beyond my own family and friends. Why should my own circle have the sole delight of my foreign cooking? This new book of international recipes was difficult in its compilation only in the task of deciding what should not be included.

Mmm, Judy mused. Simplicity. That's what I want. And variety and excellence. Maybe I can use this and get somewhere with Roger. She read on:

> Really good cooking is both imaginative and creative, as well as tasting *good*. And the best is not technically difficult. Patience, guidance and encouragement can transform the ordinary cook into one of the highest order. To be a chef is to be a professional with years of training and even decades of practice. That is not the requirement for a top flight home-cook. A basic knowledge of the standard techniques of the kitchen, together with techniques I have learned from experience, is all that is required. This is the book for you.

Judy paused, her finger saving her place on the page. "Years of training"? she thought. It's as if *I've* had years of training, and at least a decade of practice. Chef I am not, according to Roger. But – "top flight home-cook". Surely that could be me.

"A basic knowledge of the standard techniques of the kitchen."
By now I'd have to have *that,* whatever Roger says. And what
else?

> The ingredients for these recipes are readily available at home.
> Most will be in your kitchen cupboard right now. You may need to
> shop for the more exotic herbs and spices.

She made a slight noise, signifying agreement, then turned
the pages again, coming across the heading: "Basic Kitchen
Equipment":

> *Jars for Storage:* Glass jars, small and with screw tops, will
> readily house dried herbs and spices; fresh herbs in a large airtight
> jar will keep well.
> *Knives:* To save time and temper, very sharp knives and a firm
> chopping block are essential.
> *Cooking Vessels:* A boiler, a skillet – and a crockpot may be useful.

She turned to the section labelled "Kitchen Tips", running
her eye down the page:

> *Butter:* real butter should be the rule, whenever possible.
> Margarine should never be used, unless (at a pinch) containing ten
> per cent butter. Never, when frying, use margarine.
> *Sauces:* if you don't want lumps, add hot liquid. With milk sauces,
> this is of primary importance.

Judy Melton nodded approvingly. *I* don't think I make
lumpy sauces or curdled salad dressing. But Roger does. He's
always complaining about lumps in the sauce or the custard,
and fussing about my salads. I'll show him.

Grasping the book firmly under her arm she hurried toward
the counter at the front of the shop. She spoke to the owner,
perched on a stool, idly reading a book open in front of him.
He looked up briefly. "You can have it for $5.00," he said
seeming not even to glance at the volume. "Cook books. Dime
a dozen these days. Take it or leave it, lady." She took it.

Outside, in the car, she looked again at the index. Recipes
from Australia and New Zealand, the Balkans, Russia, Swit-
zerland. Creole cooking. You name it, it was there. She sighed
in satisfaction. Tonight, yes, tonight for the first time she might
produce something Roger actually *liked*. She paused. Something he doesn't complain about, anyway.

"Judy! Judy! Ju-dy! What is this?" The call came from the diningroom. She took a deep breath and braced herself. Could he possibly have found anything wrong with *this* meal? She had tried carpet-bag steak from *The Cook's Encyclopædia,* thinking she could not go wrong. "Ju-dy!" The voice was even more insistent. She went.

"What *is* this, Judy? A man's got to eat." He was halfway through the steak before he had yelled, she noticed. That, at least, was an advance.

"It's carpet-bag steak, Roger. A new recipe from an old recipe book I found. They say it's easy to do, but should taste good. It's oysters and mushrooms and parsley and lemon..." She knew she was babbling now, with disappointment and frustration, and even fright. When he got into a rage, she never knew what he might do. He was pretty noisy when something happened he didn't like. He shouted and yelled. And worse.

This time, he picked up the plate and waved it about. "When are you going to learn to cook, woman? How long is it going to take? Judy, Judy. What's a man going to do with you? Just what *is* he going to do?"

As suddenly it had begun, his voice subsided. He put the plate back on the table. He lifted his knife and fork, cutting into the remainder of the steak. Judy imperceptibly shrugged. It seemed it was all over – for now, at least. The sound of the knife scratching on the plate was replaced by the sound of masticating jaws. Roger's jaws. She looked at him, then sat at her side of the table and began eating from her own plate. Certainly, it looked all right to her. But she was unable to judge whether or not it tasted all right. She had lost all sense of her own ability to taste and enjoy. Or she did when she ate with Roger. Was he right? Was she just a hopeless cook, that nothing could change?

Later, she sat reading through *The Cook's Encyclopædia*. It was too early yet to give up. Surely she would improve over time. She should concentrate on a number of recipes. Sufficient to keep a variety for Roger's meals, but not so many that she could not reach a good standard. Surely she could reach a good standard? Miranda Davidson was convinced anyone with basic cooking skills could use the book, and turn out – an *excellent* cook.

She leafed through to Austria. She would try Austria soon, she resolved, looking at a recipe for chicken stuffing. She made notes in a pad on the table by her side, listing the ingredients. Eight ounces of cooked chopped chicken meat. Two ounces of butter. One and a half ounces of flour. Three quarters of a pint of white stock or milk. Two ounces of mushrooms. Salt. Pepper. And the directions were not too difficult. What did Miranda Davidson say?

Gently saute the mushrooms and chicken for exactly five minutes in the butter. Remove them from the butter and keep them hot. Make a roux with the butter and flour, add the heated stock gradually.

Surely that would keep Roger happy. She couldn't do anything to spoil that recipe, surely. She went on through the book, deciding on the next week's dinners.

Dessert? Well, there was an easy one for Austria, just right to go with the chicken. Apple pudding: "Peel, slice and core one and a half pounds of cooking apples. Stew gently…"

Mmm, she wondered, reading on. Maybe it's more difficult than I thought. Canary milk. What on earth's that? She turned back to the recipe, at page twenty-seven. Another read-through, then she nodded. It was not really hard at all. Just milk, an egg yolk, castor sugar and vanilla. A good one to try, Roger liked apples so much. She flipped further, to China and Japan. "Chinese Pork with Mushrooms", she read. "Eat hot or cold – when it will be a thick jelly." She looked up for a moment, wondering.

For Roger, hot, not cold. No thick jelly for him. At least, not for a main course. Jelly for dessert, yes. Jelly for dinner, no.

She moved on, reaching France this time. Ox Tongue with Mushrooms. Mmm. The recipe was a bit more complicated. Three processes to follow, as well as soaking the tongue for twelve hours in cold water before even beginning. But Roger always raved when his mother made tongue. Judy had tried Mrs Roberson's recipe, but it had never seemed to work. Maybe now, with Miranda Davidson's direction, it would work.

There were lots of good vegetable recipes in the section on France. Roast onions. Easy. Glazed turnips: twelve small, very young turnips; one pint of boiling salted water; one teaspoon castor sugar; two ounces of butter. She would have to be very careful. "Cook very slowly till the sauce turns brown and sticky. Do not burn." She would turn them just right, so as not to let the stickiness stick – to the bottom of the pan. Miranda Davidson's technique should do the trick.

India. Well, Roger liked curries. At least, he did when they went to friends' homes for dinner. Susan Renshaw had made one that Roger had raved about for days. Weeks, even. She had tried it, but without success. Just the same old: "Ju-dy. What *is* this?" But, with Miranda Davidson at hand, maybe, this time, it would go right. "Vindaloo Curry", she read. What about adding a few mushrooms?

Miranda Davidson was strong on making sure that if one did alter the recipes, the results should not go under her title. Yoghurt substituted for cream? Perfectly proper, but the dish should not bear the traditional name:

> An approximation to *boeuf stroganoff* can be made with yoghurt, but it is not the real thing. Not to recognise this is to debase the great classic dishes, as with *sole veronique* or *crepes suzette*. Inevitably, this results in a diminution of standards.

Judy Melton could agree with that. If she put mushrooms in Vindaloo curry, it wouldn't be Vindaloo curry. But Roger generally liked mushrooms. He ate them at other people's houses. They would probably go well with the steak in the curry. She would try it, just once.

Judy Melton turned finally to the back of the book. Spain. She leafed through the pages, keeping an eye out for something which might please Roger. Lamb kidneys with white wine, she read, pausing. That might do it. Button mushrooms. Four slices of bacon. A quarter of a pint of white wine. Parsley. Salt. Pepper.

Dessert? Spanish fritters. "Cut the crusts off four slices of white bread and cut into fingers one inch wide..."

Easy, she thought, shutting her notebook and *The Cook's Encyclopædia*. Time to get down to business.

She drove out into the country the following morning, early, before doing the shopping. Most ingredients she had. Cinnamon. Butter. Salt and pepper. White wine. Parsley and mint grew in the garden, near the tap at the back of the house and at the side of the shed and garage. But she needed other items, too.

She had plumped for Chinese tonight, a new start, putting to the back of her mind Roger's reaction to the carpet-bag steak. She was impressed with Miranda Davidson's ideas on Chinese and Japanese cooking:

> Chinese and Japanese cooking is an art that will not be mastered until you consciously adopt an Eastern way of thinking. Western ideas are not attuned to the Eastern concept of time. Forget your Western haste and adapt to a different rhythm.

Yes, Judy thought. Time to forget my Western notions. She noted that soy sauce was the basis, according to Miranda Davidson, of Asian cookery. No need to take up the admixture of chemicals, with soy sauce on hand, wrote the cooking pundit.

That suited Judy Melton. Simple and easy. Recipes she could do without changing her normal routine. She had no desire to work in an elaborate chemical laboratory. For her, a simple kitchen. One that could produce the *right* meals for Roger.

She was aiming at the *right* meal for tonight. And she wanted fresh ingredients. Soy sauce – Dixon Street. Easy enough to go there later today. Then she would buy pork. But this morning, she was out to collect field mushrooms. She had read the brief introduction to cooking in Australia and New Zealand, and decided to follow it to the letter, mixing the fresh air of the Antipodes with the mystery of the East:

> In these lands of sunshine and open air, the wide open spaces are replete with rich natural resources. Friendliness and hospitality, sport and outdoor life makes everyone a hearty eater.

This had led her thoughts to a paddock not far away, where she had often gone with school friends, collecting mushrooms. An hour and a half to drive there and back. It would clear her head, preparing her for getting things right for Roger's evening meal. Field mushrooms are much better than mushrooms from the shop. Anyway, she hoped so. And she hoped there would be some there, growing where she could find them. She didn't want to have to hurry. That would be quite contrary to adopting the "Eastern way of thinking". She drove on.

The field was still there. As before, mushrooms thrust their smoothly rounded white heads through the brown earth. Judy Melton bent down, a cardboard carton in one hand, picking as she went. Through her head ran the lessons of childhood. Agaricus, the mushroom with the brown gills, and perfectly good for cooking. Amanita, the mushroom that looked identical to Agaricus, except for its white gills. And deadly poisonous. She must make sure she collected the correct ones.

She walked lightly over the paddock. There were so many. Clearly children didn't come here any more. Or perhaps they came later on, after school. She would collect enough not only for Chinese pork and mushrooms, but for the ox tongue with mushrooms à la France, too. And what about trying carpet-bag steak again. And going through the book, she had noted mushrooms and sour cream, a dish from Poland. Perhaps she could add that, as well, sometime. As a side dish.

She stood for a moment, looking over towards the edge of the clearing, where a fence divided the paddock from a small stream. The carton was almost full. She could fit in a few dozen more, then that was it. She bent again.

The dinner table was set. She had added mushroom soup to the menu. True to the dictate of Miranda Davidson, she had not involved herself in too much preparation. She had resorted to packet soup. But surely this was acceptable, just once, she thought, recalling the words of *The Cook's Encyclopædia*, not to be too ambitious or over-enthusiastic. One new dish only, per meal. No heat-and-flustering in the kitchen for the students of Miranda Davidson.

Soup from a packet needed no last-minute preparation. She wanted to concentrate on the main course.

Fruit and cheese, Judy had thought when she planned the meal, three courses written into her note book. Chinese pork with mushrooms is my ambitious main dish. It'll be cheese at the end, no dessert this time.

The cheese board stood already in the alcove, a goodly wedge of a green pepper cheese astride it, breathing. Roger had a weakness for good cheeses. Would he appreciate her taste this time?

"A good cook's essential quality is a taste for good food," wrote Miranda Davidson: "An appreciative audience will be yours if you like good food, and are prepared to take a little trouble in preparing it."

Judy Melton had certainly "taken a little trouble". Traipsing about the paddocks for an hour or so. Buying just the right soy sauce, a deep, deep brown, colouring the pork and mushrooms with a splendid dark richness. Even the soup, with its complement of added, fresh mushrooms, was done to perfection.

She was jolted back into the present. "Judy! Ju-dy!..." Roger's voice rang out from the diningroom. Her head jerked up. Picking up the cheese board, she walked out of the kitchen, down the short hallway, and in to confront Roger.

"What is this, Judy? What are you serving me up now? I've drunk the soup. Passable. Just passable. But what could anyone do with soup anyway. Even you. But this, this..." He indicated with a hand towards his plate, piled high with pork and mushrooms, swimming in soy sauce. "What do you think I am," he cried. "Man or beast?" She sank into her chair as he took up his fork, plunging it toward his plate to spear a large piece of pork and an even larger piece of mushroom. She watched as he directed it toward his gaping mouth, then ferried it inside. His jaws closed. He began chomping. She looked at her plate and moved pieces of pork and mushroom around on it. She raised her fork and ate a cube of pork.

"Mrs Melton. Mrs Melton." She was conscious of an unknown voice talking to her through a haze. Slowly, she opened her eyes. Where was she? She looked at a hand that was lying on a white, white sheet. Slowly she became aware that it was her hand. She looked up. The walls around her were white. No, they were not walls. They were white curtains, hung on tracks and pulled around the bed where she was lying.

"Where am I?" she asked. Her voice hardly seemed to belong to her. She felt disorientated. She looked at the man who was sitting on the bed, quite close to her. Just behind him, to his left, stood a woman dressed in white.

"I'm Dr Danbury, Dr Tom Danbury, Mrs Melton," he said. He held her hand. Hers looked very pale and very small in his large brown one. She looked up at him.

"Mrs Melton, you've been in hospital for two days now. You and Mr Melton came in by ambulance at about 5.00 AM on Tuesday morning." He paused for a short moment, then went on.

"You kept your head commendably, Mrs Melton. Apparently you and your husband woke at about 4.30 AM with terrible pains. You phoned the hospital. Casualty. They sent someone around at once. Dr Trent and I have been looking after you ever since."

Judy waited for him to continue.

"It's important for you to rest, Mrs Melton, and you'll be out of here in no time. Food poisoning. We've done tests, and I'm afraid it was the mushrooms…"

He hesitated, glancing at her to make sure she was all right, then said, "Soy sauce. Even if anyone could tell the difference between Agaricus and Amanita, the soy sauce would make them look normal…brown…anyway. No way of knowing."

He paused again. She waited, wondering.

"And…and I'm afraid I have bad news about Mr Melton, too. He passed away twelve hours ago. I'm sorry, Mrs Melton. This is usually the case where food poisoning's concerned. If two people eat the same food, it usually hits the man harder than it does the woman. Men eat more, you know."

She closed her eyes. Dr Danbury put his cool hand on her brow.

"It's not your fault, Mrs Melton. It was the mushrooms. You mustn't blame yourself. It had absolutely nothing to do with your cooking, nothing."

She felt him rise from the bed.

"You must get some sleep. Just rest. If you want anything, press the buzzer on the wall, here. Sister Marshall is on duty, and Nurse Reid here will come at once. Just rest, Mrs Melton."

She sensed him moving away, then heard his rubber soled shoes squeaking over the shining floor. She sighed and turned her head to the pillow.

She was alone. Dr Danbury and the nurse had gone. Nothing to do with my cooking. He says, she thought. His words hung on the air. They seemed to echo around the room as she lay, her face hidden.

Roger would have something different to say. Wherever he is, up there or down below, I can *hear* him saying: Judy, what *was* that...It's your bad cooking.

She lay a moment more, a smile creeping slowly on to her features. A smile that would not stop. A smile hidden from view.

Of course, she added softly to herself. Roger. And Dr Danbury. They're both wrong.

High Art

AT THE ART Gallery on North Terrace, just along from Kintore Avenue, Claudia King had begun a stocktake, deep in the nether reaches of the basement, of the Gallery's holdings. Christopher Semple, the Director, had chosen her for her conscientiousness and devotion to detail.

No imagination, that girl, he declared to himself. But she'll get the job done if anyone will. It had been waiting for years, he knew. And if he didn't make use of Claudia and her plodding but particular style right now, she might leave, and he would be left with a cellar full of paintings, not knowing what they were, who painted them, who donated them, from whence they came. Time to get on top of the basement, he thought. And Claudia King was just the girl for it.

Claudia knew precisely what Christopher Semple thought of her. Mostly, it didn't worry her. It allowed her to get on with her work (and her own painting, in private) without him fussing and prodding and pushing and carrying on, as he so often did with the other curators. And any of the staff, for that matter.

Down in the basement she was even more out of his range. He simply left her to it, and she got on with it. Coming in every morning at 8.00 AM, she perked a pot of coffee and took it with her, downstairs, where she had smuggled in a hot plate. She kept the heat and liquid well away from the holdings. But it was there, ready for her, when she wanted a break.

Sorting and listing, Claudia worked through the sculpture and paintings, remarking to herself first on the hideousness of this item, then on the outlandishness of that. It seemed that the basement was cramped with the art no one wanted, now.

Purchased, no doubt, by some earlier Director full of his own importance and ability to foresee the future: they all thought they were the magicians or prophets of the art world, with the ability to ferret out the next Gauguin, the potential Sydney Nolan, the hidden Norman Lindsey, the Auguste Renoir or Pablo Picasso waiting on the horizon to be identified, then lauded and applauded, fêted and festooned.

Here and there she came upon a prize piece, a rolled canvas that had gone out of fashion and been left to gather dust, and which revealed a once little known painter, now grown great. Or, sometimes, a work she prized, signed by Margaret Preston or Ethel Spower, or some other woman artist who was only now being recognised as worthy. Or Claudia saw talent, whatever might be the judgement of critic and pundit. The years of failed recognition, of no encouragement, of ridicule they had suffered. She thought of Germaine Greer's *Obstacle Race* and Janine Burke's *Australian Women Artists*, rushing home, sometimes, to leaf through the pages looking, looking, looking for paintings or names that might be familiar, hoping that her foray into the basement might find some prize. A friend sent her a copy of Carol Ambrus' *Ladies' Picture Show*, a source book on Australian women painters over the last century. Claudia took it in to the gallery, keeping it beside her as she sifted and sorted, dusted and catalogued.

She saw it now, the exhibition of the year, "Discoveries from the Vault: An Exhibition of Australia's Heritage, Women Artists". The queues would stretch for miles down North Terrace. The show would break all records. It would go on tour, to all capital cities, with her as curator. She would hunt out background information on these newly discovered artists, and deliver an erudite evening lecture before the hordes were set free to roam the rows and rows of fine Australian art. If she were brave, she could include some of her own paintings. They were good, she knew. But the climate for women in the art world remained cold. Exhibit her own? Where would she find a gallery brave enough to devote its walls to a one woman show? Where would she find a gallery with the courage to defy the critics, those devotees of the pen – and male art.

Fine Australian women's art. Fine Australian artists. Lots of them about. In attics and basements. Little doubt of that. Her work, after all, was secreted in the Gallery basement, smuggled in to put to good use the temperature and protection of a professionally designed space. Even if it were in the depths, rather than exhibited for the crowds.

Once, Claudia King had aspirations to be a *recognised* fine Australian artist. Before she learnt that there was art – and "women's art". Before she learned it was all in the name: Bruno or Peter or Clarence or Claude. Beryl and Petra and Clarissa – and Claudia – were "out".

Born into the family of a railway fettler father and house cleaning mother, she had little chance of realising the dream. But she tried. A teacher at the local school at Naracoorte encouraged her talent for drawing, and she managed to cadge pencils and paper and charcoal sticks from her for two years, between the ages of nine and eleven. Then Miss Nelson left, to be replaced by Mrs Donald, who would not countenance "wasting time drawing", as she put it. Mr West, the headmaster, frowned on it too, having no sympathy for her when he came upon her sitting outside the classroom one day, where she had been sent by Mrs Donald as a penance for drawing in class.

Claudia made friends with Kerry MacIntosh, the daughter of the local newsagent-cum-general store manager. Fortuitously, it turned out that Kerry had all the pencils and papers she wanted, and more. The more she passed on to Claudia. In the afternoons, after school, when the other kids had sneaked off down to the river to smoke (and choke on) cigarettes filched from their parents, Kerry and Claudia set themselves up in the paddocks and fields around Naracoorte, paper and pencils in front of them, sketching and shading with an earnestness born of a desire to take themselves (and to be taken) seriously.

She and Kerry went on to High School together, travelling on the local school bus. They sat down the back and taught themselves to draw in a moving vehicle, with school kids screaming and shouting on all sides. They rested their sketching pads on the ledge between the rear bench seat and the back window, and drew the receding hills, or the passing wheat fields, or the lumbering trucks and trailers that followed them down the road.

They graduated to watercolours, then to oils. But the expense was crippling to a railway fettler's daughter. Claudia's mother took in more washing and ironing, and did more house cleaning, but it never seemed to be enough. It was not only the need for the paints, but there was the special paper, a palette, cleaning fluids. An easel. Claudia and Kerry took kitchen chairs out into the fields, or to the side of the road, where each set up by leaning a large piece of flat wood against a chairback, affixing the paper with the butterfly clips Mrs MacIntosh put in her hair, nightly, to give a perky kink to the waves of her perm.

At fifteen, Claudia left school. She got a job at the Mac-Intosh's newsagency, taking the greater proportion of the wages she was left, after paying her parents board, in sketching pads, and paper, watercolours and (when she was feeling really extravagant) oils. She lasted two years. Then she told her mother, who told her father, that she was moving to the city, to Adelaide. There had to be something more to life than Naracoorte.

"Still got this mad artist bug in her, John," said Mrs King to her husband. "Thinks that if she goes to Adelaide, she might be able to get enough money together to enrol at the Technical College to study art."

"What's there to study about *art?*" exploded Mr King. "The girl's a fool. Wasting all that time drawing on bits of paper and sloshing paint here and there. Make more sense for her to learn how to paint houses. Or even cars, for that matter." He paused, looking at Mrs King for guidance. "At least she might get paid for it, mother," he snorted.

Claudia went to live in Adelaide, working first in Coles as a sales assistant, where she graduated to manager of the stationery department. She saved what money she could, putting it into an account labelled "Art School". Then she landed a job at Kinloch's in Tynte Street, North Adelaide, selling art supplies. Like all the staff, she was allowed paints and paper at fifty per cent reduction. On the weekends and Monday holidays she would take the tram down to Glenelg, painting on the beach and in the sand dunes. In lunch hours she hunted around the city for indoor locations she could use for rainy days. She managed to obtain permission to set up her easel (she had saved for, and bought, a real one now: no more kitchen chairs for her) in Parliament House, in the Town Hall, and in the Supreme Court. In all three there were endless angles and views, siderooms and entrances, stairways and stairwells she could sketch and paint. The interiors of the buildings had remained so since they were built, and they retained their ancient (for Australian anglo-settlement) flavour. She painted herself back into those early years, empathising with earlier artists, but adopting her own distinctive style.

After two years of saving hard, Claudia King applied for and was accepted into the technical college. She was off to Art School. She managed to do two years full-time, keeping her job at Kinloch's, working holidays and Saturday mornings, and Thursday night shopping when it came in. Shortly after, she secured her first position at the Gallery, and studied part-time. When she finished, doing the last year over two years, she jumped at the chance when one of the curators left, and she filled the vacancy.

As she had since coming to Adelaide, for two weeks, at Christmas, she returned to Naracoorte, taking her paints and brushes, and going off in the mornings and afternoons to the river where she spent lazy, but industrious, hours. She had fallen out of touch with Kerry MacIntosh. The MacIntoshes had long since moved on, their store being demolished and replaced with a large modern barn of a building, combining chemist goods with newspapers and Darrell Lea chocolates and licorice. But on one of the trips back home her mother passed to her a card, recently arrived, from Kerry. Kerry was living in Melbourne and studying fine arts at Melbourne University. She was searching around for a topic for her thesis, and had half fixed on writing about the Heidelberg School. Not the men. There were women painters at that time, too, she wrote to Claudia in her long-forgotten yet familiar hand. "Funny how the women seem always to be left out, isn't it?" she ended.

"But of course I've got to get my topic through the powers-that-be, and they're not a progressive lot here. Looks like I'll probably be stuck with writing about some man, or group of men. Oh well!"

She added a PS: "Let me know what you think. Any ideas?"

Claudia King and Kerry MacIntosh were back in touch again. They exchanged letters regularly, sometimes writing long accounts of what each was doing, sometimes sending scrappy notes, just to keep in touch. Sometimes the time lapses between letters lengthened into months for both of them. On other occasions they wrote more often, only a few weeks separating each missive.

Sometimes, they telephoned one another, across the vast expanse of land between Adelaide and Melbourne. When Claudia suffered bouts of self-doubt, the feeling that she was "only a woman artist", not a "real" painter, she talked with Kerry. And Kerry got her painting again, believing in herself. Now, Claudia was producing work she could hardly fault, herself. And she was her most savage critic. More savage than those male teachers at Tech, who saw the young men in their classes as the new breed, the new up-and-coming, the hopes of the Australian art world. So savage that sometimes it was difficult to cling to what she knew with that certainty born of real talent, that she was good.

And appreciating the support, the unsentimental, critical yet caring response from Melbourne-based Kerry, Claudia King reciprocated in responding to telephone calls from Melbourne to Adelaide. Kerry had self-doubts, too. About her ability to write. Her knowledge of art. Her capabilities as an analyst of art history, styles, schools, painters. Sometimes, she simply needed someone who appreciated her talent to support her in her knowledge that although in disagreement with everyone, but everyone, in the department, she *was* right. She was not mad. Her approach, her instincts were sound.

Kerry was having problems with her thesis. "Male chauvinist sods," she wrote. "Wouldn't know a woman artist if they fell over one. As far as they're concerned, they're all spinsters and maiden aunts dabbling amongst the flowers, the dawns, the sunsets and the bushes, waiting for the prince in shining armour to arrive, white charger in tow, then they'll throw over the pots and the paints and the brushes, and replace them gladly, lovingly with the pots and the pans. And endless picking up of wet towels from bathroom floors!"

It looked as if she was losing her battle for devoting her thesis to a woman artist. Well, second best would be taking up some unknown male. Overlooked. Forgotten. Next best. Bearable. She didn't really think so. But she wanted the degree. She needed it. She had to qualify to go on – to – what? Teaching art in a university that thought of women artists and women critics as a race apart, a secondary breed, an irrelevance?

Claudia knew for sure that Kerry had lost when Christopher Semple came on one of his rare visits to the basement, flapping a letter in his hand.

"Just received this from some student at Melbourne," he said peremptorily putting himself in front of a grimy looking frame, painting grubby but intact, Claudia had just set up before her, and was regarding with concentrated interest. "Says she's researching some fellow – Clifford – Clifford Wright...No, Clifford Reines." He paused, flapping the letter at her again and poking at it with his right index finger.

"Clifford Reines. Never heard of him. But she says he's a member of the Heidelberg School." Christopher Semple's voice dropped reverentially when he uttered The Term, as it had come to be known in Claudia's head. It was the same with everyone. Gallery directors, art critics, the "educated public". Talk about the art of the Heidelberg lot and before you knew it, grown men were acting like small boys. The only other time that was true was with Sunday and John Reid. Talk about "Sunday and John" (or "John and Sunday" as it more often was put), and grown men were at it, dropping their voices – and almost dropping to their knees.

Christopher Semple, urbane man of the world, creator of himself, director of art (no mere critic, he) was clearly impressed. His right hand went instinctively to his throat. There it located the Windsor knot that had become his trademark, together with the tie itself: long, broad triangle of pale and dark blue striped silk. "Oxford man" it screamed to those "in the know". And after all they were the only ones who counted.

He had gone to Oxford, once. For a year. Quite sufficient time to purchase not one tie, but ten, and to effect the odd inflection of voice that distinguished him, as he had come to believe, from the parvenus and philistines inhabiting the world of art. If he could get them out of *his* world, he would. But then there wouldn't be many left...And after all, it was a business this. Had to have them coming to the openings and closings, the exhibitions and the festivals. Bums on seats. Feet on parquet floors. Ah well, that was the name of the game nowadays.

He brought himself back to the present. And Claudia King.

"Thinks it may be that there are paintings in our holdings that have been forgotten, hidden away. Unfashionable for a long time, of course, and may have been stashed in the basement."

He prodded the letter again.

"She's written to the galleries in each of the capital cities, but thinks there's most chance with us and Victoria, because they mostly worked over there, but some of them came west to the Adelaide hills as well. Thinks this Reines might have worked here for a bit, left paintings behind. Might have been caught up in some auction or other, and ended up here. In our Gallery."

He meant *his* Gallery. The pronoun was in the royal collective form.

Claudia looked interested and intelligent, although in the instant of doing so, she realised it would be lost on Chris.

She automatically called him Chris. She couldn't help it. He *looked* such a Chris. Elongating his name at Oxford (when picking up the voice and ties) didn't make the difference he hoped. Left Australia Chris, and returned Christopher, as did so many men, back then. Jim to James. Dick to Richard. But they remained – themselves.

He went on, not expecting her to speak. "Just take the letter, will you, and file it. If you come across anything by Reines, you can let her know." He turned to go.

"Oh, think she says she's coming across later this month, anyway, and wants to come in. We can let her have a bit of a look around. Just see to it, will you. Got a good reference from Professor Bisquith. Clark Bisquith, of course. Can't go past that."

He thrust the letter into her hand, and left.

Old boys at it again, thought Claudia. Once you've got their approval, you're in all right.

She knew she had guessed right (although she didn't really have to guess) when she looked down at the letter. The signature was familiar. "Kerry MacIntosh." It would be good to see her again.

In Melbourne, the art critics waxed lyrical. (Melbourne, after all, was the home of the Heidelberg School. Melbourne always supported its own.) The *Age* arts page was awash on the day the exhibition opened:

UNDER GOLDEN SKIES

Clifford Reines' masterpieces stand on their own. They have that special quality that comes only rarely into public view. Every brush stroke is evidence of an artistic hand roaming free under the controlled but not controlling force of an outstanding, yet modest, intellect...

These twelve paintings, recently brought back from a past which had too rudely forgotten them, stand also as a toast to the Heidelberg School, to the inspired efforts of artists working to create a new genre...

But Reines is not an imitator of his own Movement. His works have that unique quality, the quality of the artist who knows who he is. He surpasses Roberts and Streeton. He stands alone. No one could doubt the quality, the intrinsic worth, of this fine talent. The Adelaide Art Gallery – Christopher Semple himself – stands commended for bringing Clifford Reines back to the world.

The rapturous tones were easily matched by those of the *Australian*'s art critic, who covered the exhibition initially in Adelaide, then toured with it, recording his reactions as he viewed the collection anew in each capital city. In Sydney he wrote:

EXHIBITION OF INSPIRATION TO BE
FOUND UNDER GOLDEN SUMMER SKIES

As I walked along Domain Road toward the Art Gallery, my mind drifted back to that afternoon in Adelaide, four months ago, when I walked up the grey stone steps of the Gallery in North Terrace, toward the Clifford Reines "Summers" exhibition. Four months? All at once it seemed ten years, yet only days, ago.

What can one say, of an artist whose works have lain, dustily forgotten, in the bowels of a temple to art? What can one say, of the works that now bring hope, and joy, and inspiration to a new generation of artists, to a new generation of art lovers, to a new public? What can be said of the artist who in the midst of being so clearly united with the Movement we know so well as the Heidelberg School, yet has his own very special quality, his own masterful touch, his very own essence and essential character.

What need be said of the Director of the Gallery who, against all odds, searched and found the prize to exceed all prizes, the works that are so fine, my breath catches in my throat...

Not to be outdone, the *Sydney Morning Herald* critic had been there, too:

PASTELS, POWER, PAINT, PERFECTION

The new exhibition at the Gallery is not to be missed. Clifford Reines, rediscovered after too long an absence, brings to the walls of the Gallery soft lights, glistening leaves, mottled wheat-fields...These works, brought anew to the world by Christopher Semple and the Adelaide Art Gallery, are worthy of the highest praise, as is Semple's perspicacity...

In Darwin, when the exhibition reached the "Top End", the *Northern Territory News* covered its front page with the critic's review. Never before had such an editorial decision been made. The art world, and even the public, loved it. The *West Australian* and the *Daily News* in Perth each ran full-page reviews, one on page three, the other as a centre liftout section, with colour prints of the paintings and an order form to be filled out and posted off, with the extra admonishment that there were limited copies available. The *Courier Mail* was full of "Clifford Reines: In Brisbane". When the exhibition made its way back to Adelaide, via Canberra and the National Gallery, the *Canberra Times* in its Friday edition published a

119

page of reviews by four or five critics; the Sunday edition gave pride of place in the arts pages to a review by a New York critic who had come out especially to see "Clifford Reines. The National Gallery Exhibition".

Kerry MacIntosh was well pleased. She noted, ruefully, that her researches had been laid at the feet of Christopher Semple. She need not have existed. The days, and weeks, she spent together with Claudia sitting in the cellars under the Gallery, churning up the dust, then dusting off new laid dust here, rubbing off apparent grime there, eyeing critically that canvas, squinting to read the signature...Then the rush of appreciation when (Christopher Semple conveniently happening to be in the basement at the time, prodding Claudia about some minor matter) the batch of ten was found. All together, one atop the other, stacked away in what happened to be the darkest corner of the basement. Clifford Reines! She had whooped with excitement. Christopher Semple had added his applause, spontaneously, without realising, at first, that as Director he ought not to be cheering in the cellar with a student and a junior curator. Claudia had joined in, laughing. Then they had gone on to find two more, hidden even more obscurely, between a door which led into a broad corridor that had been built, obviously, to keep the cold and the damp from whatever was stored there. Christopher Semple grabbed them up, holding them first to his chest, then at arms length, squinting one eye and breathing hard.

The find was taken over totally by the Gallery. By the Director. Christopher Semple strode along the concrete floor, looking serious, while they rushed upstairs behind him, bubbling with the excitement of the discovery. He had been sceptical, at first, when Kerry had drawn his attention to the find. His mind had been on Claudia and whatever it was for which he had come down to call her to task. But impressed, always, with the thought which remained ever present, in the back of his mind, influencing (as well, he thought, it should) his view of this woman art student from Melbourne: she came complete with reference from Professor Clark Bisquith! He had grabbed whatever he could, and told the others to bring the rest. Carefully. No tripping on the basement steps, he had admonished, taking them two at a time. And panting.

Press releases were drawn up, then held off from release when the Director determined that rather than break upon the world before the paintings were properly catalogued, restored, displayed, set forth for exhibition, he would mount the exhibition to end all exhibitions. (Claudia he set to do the restoration and the curating. He didn't want anyone in on this who might take the front stage. Christopher Semple wanted it all to himself. Claudia was pliable. Claudia was grateful for whatever she could get. She would work hard. She did.)

"Clifford Reines – Banishing the Banishment, in Adelaide." No, it didn't sound quite right. "Back from the Past: Clifford Reines Artist." At last, he fixed on "Clifford Reines". Plain, sharp, and to the point. Not to be missed.

The exhibition certainly was not missed. They poured in, in their thousands. Although it was announced that the exhibition would make an Australia-wide tour, art patrons, critics, writers, painters, artists, the public – flooded into Adelaide from all points. They came from abroad. The word went out to New York, London, Bonn, Paris, Moscow. Even the Russians, full of their "glasnost" and "perestroika" came running. Two critics (they seemed to travel in pairs, these writers from the eastern block) followed the exhibition from Adelaide to Perth, to Melbourne, to Sydney. Critics swooped in from Europe and the States, drinking up the works with their eyes, praising with their pens, imploring northern hemisphere galleries to bid for a place on the tour schedule.

Kerry MacIntosh wrote the background notes on Clifford Reines. Kerry MacIntosh was the only one who knew anything about him, after all. Together with prints of the paintings and a short note saying they would hear more, she sent copies back to her parents, living in comfortable retirement north of Brisbane. She had begun writing her thesis, centred around Clifford Reines, but not so much on the man himself. More on the issues surrounding the discovery, the way in which the find was leapt upon by the art world, the manner in which art, apparently once forgotten and consigned to the dust and the cobwebs, can be recaptured as extraordinary, special, *the* find. If painted by a man, of course. Women's art remained there, and discovery was out of the question.

As she worked on, she began to wonder if she should change to political science. Or at least have a political scientist as one of the assessors of the thesis.

"Women's Art Movement", the women's gallery down towards the end of Rundle Street, was preparing for a seige. Six months on, the Clifford Reines' exhibition had settled down to its permanent place in the Adelaide Gallery. But it was about to travel overseas. The New York Institute of Art had negotiated a deal with Christopher Semple and his board of governors, for the paintings to be on show for ten days. The insurance fees were enormous. Cartage from Adelaide to New York was exorbitant. The fee to be paid to the Gallery was stupendous. But the New York Institute *wanted* Clifford Reines. And Clifford Reines it would get.

But back to Women's Art Movement. Theirs was an exhibition with far more modest a fee structure. Minimal cartage. Insurance? Well, that was the major expense. They realised that when the storm broke, and break it would, they would be sitting on either a gold mine or a spurting volcano. And either way, insurance, let's face it, was essential. They insured. And well.

The exhibition? The title came to them collectively as they sat around a table at the women's gallery, drinking herb tea and munching on muesli cookies. Home made. "Claudia King – or Clifford Reines." No question mark at the end. Just a plain, solid, firm and definite full-stop. Because there was no question, really. Once you knew. And they knew.

Kerry MacIntosh had done the background notes for this exhibition, too. (Claudia was, of course, far more real to her than Clifford Reines.) Notes on Claudia's background. Her growing up in Naracoorte, drawing, sketching, painting with minimal resources. Working hard through the years leading up to Art School, and producing some of her best work. Painting through her holidays, days off from the Gallery. The difficulty in finding somewhere to store her art. The greater difficulty in finding exhibition space. The problems she confronted in being a woman in a world peopled by men who saw only themselves. Who saw women as invisible.

In no way was it a sob story. It just told it how it was. How it was for artists who received little encouragement but whose persistence and belief in themselves pushed them on. She wove in several quotations from *The Obstacle Race* and *The Ladies' Picture Show*. She quoted Germaine Greer:

> "A woman knows that she is to be womanly and she also knows that for a drawing or a painting to be womanish is contemptible. The choices are before her: to deny her sex, and become an honourary man, which is an immensely costly proceeding in terms of psychic energy, or to accept her sex and with it second place, as the artist's consort, in fact or in fantasy."

She wrote of Claudia's response to that choice. That she had not denied her sex in her painting. That she had accepted her sex but not taken second place. If she had compromised at all, it was to become "an honourary man" in title only. And for a limited time. The time was now up.

She concluded with an invitation to the viewers, and the critics, to walk around to North Terrace and the Gallery, and to compare Claudia King's exhibition with the standing exhibition of Clifford Reines' work. "Celebration of Difference – or of the same master strokes?" ran the last line in the catalogue. (Kerry MacIntosh deliberately left in the word "master". She used it in a conscious way, determined that "master" would be accepted and read as sex-neutral. Claudia's work was masterful. Indeed, it had already been recognised by the critics as such! If only the critics realised. As they soon would.)

For when they accepted the invitation, taking the walk around to the Gallery and Clifford Reines, they would not be able to refuse the truth reflected in their eyes. Would the papers then read "Hoax of the Century?" Would the New York Institute of Art cancel the Clifford Reines' exhibition? Would the critics recover themselves by denying their own newspaper columns, their own words of less than a year old? Would Clifford Reines be buried again, in the metaphorical grave of Claudia King?

Christopher Semple's right hand nervously attacked his tie. His face was red. His voice agitated. "You no longer work here, understand? You are no longer employed. There will be no reference. And if I have anything to do with it, you will never work anywhere, anytime, in any art gallery in this country. In the world!"

His voice rose. Then it fell slightly, and he began again. "And as for your friend – your friend – Kerry – what was it? MacIntosh? You can tell her from me that her name will be mud – mud – I tell you, in every university and art institute in the un-i-verse! I'm not taking this from anyone. Being made to look a fool by a couple of women...In my own Art Gallery. MY OWN ART GALLERY." Pause. Crescendo. "You can leave now, young lady, and don't come back!"

Another breath. Then it came rushing out. "Making it all up! MAKING IT ALL UP! Treating the art world like a mob of 'don't know anythings'. Taking the critics for donkeys. Asses...No SUCH PERSON as Clifford Reines! Made up. MADE UP. Clifford Reines. Claudia King. You! You all along. Scrabbling away down in the basement there. Hiding your own work – YOUR OWN WORK. Passing it off as masterpieces. Fudging. PRETENDING you're in the same class as THE HEIDELBERG SCHOOL."

He rested for a moment against the desk, taking a breath in the midst of the tirade. "And that friend of yours. Saying she's writing a thesis. On some figment of her imagination, Clifford Reines. CLIFFORD REINES! I'll give her Clifford Reines. I'll give her writing a thesis." He glared at Claudia, almost shaking his fist. "She'll never get that thesis accepted. She'll never get it published. Writing tripe about a man who never lived, never existed. Using him as a camouflage for you. For your 'artistic' aspirations. No one will look twice at your paintings, now. The public doesn't take lightly to being made fools of."

Patronisingly, he rested a hand on her shoulder. Gently, she shrugged it off. "Well, my dear. Claudia. Or Clifford. Or whatever your name *is*. You'll never get an exhibition anywhere again. Not under the name of Claudia King, nor under the name Clifford Reines. You're out, girl. And you'd better believe it."

Bbbrrrr. Bbbbrrrr. The soft, muted tones of the pearl grey telephone sitting on the clear perspex desk in the Director's office interrupted the tirade. He grabbed the hand piece, angrily barking into it: "Hello." There was a significant pause. His tones became deferential. "Yes. Of course. Nothing important at the moment. I'll take it right now."

Clearly, he had forgotten Claudia King, who sat quietly in one of the high-backed leather chairs which Christopher Semple used for recalcitrant members of staff. Her mind drifted to Kerry MacIntosh's thesis, which had been the key to setting all this in train. The decision to take advantage of Claudia's need to smuggle her paintings into the Gallery and secrete them in the basement, where they could be stored without danger of deterioration. The need to deal effectively with the imposition on Kerry, by the powers-that-be in Fine Arts, of a thesis topic dealing with men artists, and the world of men's art. To resist the implication that there was no woman artist worthy of a dissertation. All that, together with her reading of the way women artists traditionally had been overlooked and derided, their work seen as inferior because they were women. And that it was continuing today. In art galleries, exhibitions, universities, art schools. Places of "higher learning". Repositories of taste and style, the controllers of what was "art" and what was not. What was to be viewed and what was not. What was "worthy" and what was not.

After it was all over, the secret out, the thesis (incorporating recent events) written to her satisfaction (but before submitting it) Kerry MacIntosh had transferred from the Fine Arts Department to Politics. She had decided that the thesis was wholly political. It was. And she had been awarded First Class Honours, with an offer to do her doctorate at Berkeley, in California.

Claudia came back to the present. Christopher Semple was still talking deferentially into the telephone. Well, it was not so much that he was talking, because the conversation was clearly being carried by the person on the other end of the line. But his whole body showed deference, in his stance, the hand lightly placed on the Windsor knot of his tie, the way his head was almost bowed to the sound of the voice in his ear.

"Certainly. Certainly," he now said. "I've actually got her right here with me in my office. We can organise that easily. Easily. No trouble at all. Pleased to do it." His head was now nodding rapidly to the voice on the other end of the line. "Yes. Yes. Double the fee. A royalty to the artist. First class airfare. Oh. Airfares. Yes. The other one. Yes. Yes."

The conversation came to an end. Slowly, he returned the receiver to its niche. Even more slowly, he turned to Claudia.

"New York Institute of Art on the line. Want to turn the Clifford Reines exhibition into another "Claudia King – or Clifford Reines." show. Sans question mark. Asked me to arrange with that gallery over in Rundle Street – what is it?" He effected ignorance, although after all the fuss, all the press coverage, the television cameras flooding into the exhibition space, then crowding around the steps of the Gallery to catch him and his reaction, he could hardly not know its name.

"Women's Art Movement," she said, looking at him.

"Yes. They want to put your works alongside his. That is – put the ones from Women's Art – from it alongside those we're holding here as the 'Clifford Reines Exhibition'."

He coughed, clearing his throat. Paused. Then went on, every word squeezing out between his lips like toothpaste from an empty tube, "Want that Kerry MacIntosh over there as well. And you. To front the exhibition. They're doubling the fee. Some arrangement with London, too…The Tate."

The words were almost choking him. Voice disappearing into the podgy white throat behind the Windsor-knotted tie, he added, in a line almost thrown away, hardly to be heard by Claudia. But she heard it, anyway: "Something to do with the Louvre, too. Paris end coming through, apparently."

When they flew in to New York, they were greeted by a panoply of officials and throngs of critics, journalists, artists. (All the artists were women. They understood and applauded.)

"How did you get away with it, girls?" asked the Director of the New York Institute of Art, who was first in line to greet them. (Not often did she come to greet an exhibiting artist. Not even when Salvador Dali made his final visit to the States, in the first year she held the position, did she come to the airport. Sent her second-in-command, certainly. Top hotel. Champagne on ice. Winter roses in bunches throughout the suite. But no "doorstop" greeting from the Director.)

"High art has no gender, as they say," said Kerry and Claudia together, laughing.

When Kerry MacIntosh published her book, *Art, Sex and Politics*, she dedicated it to Ippolita degli Erri, the last artist of the Modena family, degli Erri, artists fêted since the early fifteenth century. Ippolita degli Erri died in the San Marco convent in 1661.

On the frontispiece she quoted from *The Obstacle Race:*

"For literally thousands of women artists we have...only names when no names were signed, or initials which might be shared with twenty others...We may only have the words, 'was also a painter' to go on, as upon Antonia Uccello's tombstone, while every year that goes past destroys more of our heritage. If anything is to be salvaged, women by the thousands must begin to sift the archives of their own districts, turn out their own attics, haunt their own salerooms and the auctions in old houses."

In her introduction she called for the creation of a world where women could acknowledge their own paintings and be recognised. And urged women to urge their sisters to sign their own paintings, and bring them into the light.

The Silent Takeover

SHE WAS NOT sure when she realised Mr Hamilton was dispensable. It crept up on her slowly, a gradual consciousness that it was "business as usual", whether Mr Hamilton was there or not. Whether he was interstate, or overseas, as so often, these days. Or right in Melbourne. Even if he was at the plant, everything went so smoothly without him. Jacobs, the foreperson, virtually ran the factory. If Jacobs couldn't handle it, naturally she stepped in. Only occasionally was it necessary to sort out some industrial issue, and then it was usually an outburst such as happens anywhere there's a factory floor with people working too closely together. One of the framemakers would mislay a knife or a bit of beading, and accuse someone else; or a packer would step on someone's foot and an antagonism, lying in wait until the day was particularly hot, or particularly cold, or particularly miserable with rain and wind, whatever it was that set people off, sparked a retaliation. Someone ended up in the toilets or the restroom sobbing or spreading ash all over the washbasins, but it was over as soon as a firm hand came in and whatever was lost was found or replaced.

With her on the spot, no point in involving Mr Hamilton.

And the office. Quite frankly, it ran better when Mr Hamilton wasn't there. Importers listed in two of the five eggshell-blue filing cabinets under the Picasso print. Picasso from the blue period; not one of the ones with the horses teeth growing out of the women's heads, signs of the artist's misogyny. Or self-hatred: a subconscious recognition by Picasso of himself as simply unattractive, a stocky little man with a waist the same size as his hips. But the 'great man' wouldn't ever paint self-portraits with mandibular jaws and incisors hooked into his forehead. Women were easier targets.

In the next two banks of drawers, export accounts. Then "domestic matters" – Mr Hamilton's records of his overseas business trips, invoices and receipts for business equipment and machinery, telephone bills, water rates, his property records, insurance, the superannuation, his will. It was her doing, of course. When she first arrived, twenty years ago next Tuesday, there was no Picasso, no eggshell-blue filing cabinets, no glass-topped desk, no export listings; in fact few export-import records, if any. Mainly "domestics". And there hadn't been much in that file, either. Mr Hamilton had only just married, and there were few overseas jaunts in those days. He was beginning to pay off what was, for the time, a large mortgage.

Today, she reflected, not only was the business almost unrecognisable. However much it was, the mortgage had been paid off long ago and the house sold. Now it was a large two-story terrace East St Kilda. Expensive, but nothing too ostentatious. Mrs Hamilton had good taste, certainly.

Twenty years next Tuesday. That was what had set off the spark that had her musing on the operations of the office. He was overseas again. Burma, *en route* to the Great Silk Road. Or would he be in Thailand now? Whichever, when he telephoned regular as clockwork, every second day, she would be able to reassure him that things were going smoothly at this end. As always.

Time something happened, she thought. The business had expanded into *objets 'd art* as well as paintings, and with China opening up, silk and screens and terracotta warriors. Then from the Australian end, Aboriginal art was coming into its own. Prices were soaring. Some of it was getting back to the artists. Perhaps that was an avenue to follow up. All that fuss about whether the Grampians were or weren't going to stay renamed for their Aboriginal ancestry. Why not? And why not concentrate on the here and now, with the art pouring out, in ochres and browns and sepia tones, and white and black wriggling lines of lizards and snakes, and the women's camps set apart. An exhibition of Aboriginal women's art? I could get that old gasworks down the back of the plant restored, she mused. Gasworks and Aboriginal art? There must be some way of drawing the two together. She would ask Lilla at the next Women's Art Collective meeting.

The gasworks would be easy, she knew. No problem with contacting the tradespeople, signing the cheques. Some would have to be countersigned by Mrs Hamilton when Mr was away, but that was no problem. No real interest in the business, or had never shown it. Too busy running the house and the three children, but co-operative and pleasant enough on the phone. Ready to come by when the children were at school, if necessary, to finish anything Mr Hamilton had left undone.

She knew he didn't telephone Mrs Hamilton all that often when he was away. She knew, because Mrs Hamilton telephoned her to see if there was anything important, any message for her. Mrs Hamilton had said Mr Hamilton preferred calling the office because the timing was so difficult, and he wanted to keep up with the business-side. Home would go on as it always did.

Mrs Hamilton added, at the time, that of course Mr Hamilton had no doubts about the office: no hitches, bubbling along. But he wants to keep in touch, and it's the business more than me that's in his mind, she had laughed.

A sensible woman, Mrs Hamilton.

And as for Mr Hamilton. If he never appeared on the office step again, business would continue. She knew the business and the contacts. She had lined most of them up. The importers and the exporters dealt mainly with her. Her Chinese customers came for the Opera House and Darling Harbour, then hopped on planes to see whatever Melbourne had to offer. The British and the Japanese were doing that, too. So were the Americans. And a few Swedes. They came running and dropped into the office on their way home, just to make contact.

Sitting at her glass topped desk with the elegant azure vase next to the pile of papers, she could see directly into the open door of the walk-in safe. It had two sections, the large open area at the front, with the reinforced shelving for any cash or valuables kept on the premises. Then there was an inner room hidden behind it, you wouldn't know it was there unless someone told you. Storage space for those very precious relics that had to be kept at a special temperature, or preserved from the air. Contact with oxygen could be damaging. The store held them safe for the buyers.

Several Egyptian sarcophagi lay, dark, bejewelled and occidental, on the floor of the storeroom right now. The 'Gold of the Pharaohs' exhibition had been and gone, with most of the Egyptian art works selling well. But Mr Hamilton was over-ambitious in his purchase of the sarcophagi. The space wasn't needed for anything else at the moment, so it didn't matter terribly. Yet she *was* a little annoyed that he hadn't completely followed her advice. The sarcophagi (and not just one of them, but two) were the evidence of it.

Tuesday. Her eye ran down Mr Hamilton's itinerary. She had arranged it, deciding on the places of call, in accordance with Mr Hamilton's style. He nominated the countries; she located potential buyers and sellers. She found the best hotels, with the best service, the best location, and the most reasonable prices. Burma. The political problems had arisen before Mr Hamilton left, but he had been determined to go. She had thought, then, maybe he would get caught up in some student demonstration. Maybe a stray bullet...But no, he had rung-in, still hale and hearty as they said in the Victorian novels. Still well and truly ALIVE.

Enough of that. Australian businessmen just didn't get shot when abroad. She recalled one being kidnapped for weeks in Saudi Arabia. But that was the point. It was for weeks or months, perhaps. But, in the end, he came back. Just as did Mr Hamilton, after six...or was it seven weeks? Her eyes flicked to the itinerary again: six weeks and four days. He'd be back. Time was nearly up. She had to settle down to planning. Hardly efficient to rely upon soldiers or terrorists or student revolutionaries to do the job. It was time for her to act responsibly.

Poison. Certainly the easiest *modus operandi*. A few drops of cyanide in the glass of whisky she knew he would pour as soon as he came in. She had Mr Hamilton's habits down pat. Twenty years working for one person, it was inevitable that she should. Impossible that he should select a glass from a different place in the row of ten waiting for him in the liquor cabinet. He would never notice a few drops of colourless fluid at the bottom. Far too eager to up-end the bottle. And even if he did notice, he'd think it was water. What did it matter when drinking whisky and water the way he did, whether the water went in first or last? Death would be instantaneous, with a whiff of almond scent on the breath the only "give away", so long as there was no autopsy.

But there was no way of getting Mr Hamilton and his glass of scotch into the smaller storeroom, before he took the fatal slug. And this she would have to do, to have any realistic chance of success. He weighed fourteen stone. She weighed seven. She was strong and willing to lug boxes and cases about. Never needed anyone to help her shift furniture. She recalled pushing and pulling the piano of her childhood from one side of the loungeroom to the other when she was fourteen. But it had been a terrific job, and she didn't want to have to repeat it with Mr Hamilton. Besides, there was always a possibility that someone might come in, just as she dragged him over the carpet. Impossible to explain. And why should she? No. That was definitely not the way.

And cyanide in this day and age? No chance she could get it without alerting someone to her intentions. What would a perfectly respectable-looking woman of forty want with cyanide? Some chemists might not be too bright, but she couldn't see them handing cyanide over the counter without raised eyebrows at least. And wasn't there some "poisons book" that had to be signed? So Agatha Christie said. That was England, but she didn't imagine it would be any different here. Was cyanide a "prescribed drug"? No, not poison, whether cyanide or arsenic or Ratsak. Possibly easier to get, but who had rats nowadays, anyway? It had to be something quick and easy, done in the storeroom, right next to the largest sarcophagus, without Mr Hamilton suspecting anything.

She strolled over, leaning up against the door between the large division and the smaller space. Her eyes moved slowly around the tiny room, then she turned to regard the shelves in the outer area where smaller pieces were kept. She picked up one of the two gold ingots lying on the shelf second from the floor. It weighed heavily in her hand. Gently rocking backwards on her heels, experimentally she moved it from one hand to the other. Two in a sock, she thought. A very large sock. No suspicion would fall because a forty-year-old woman purchased a large pair of men's hose from the sock counter at Myers. And it would take little to lure Mr Hamilton into the storeroom. He was fascinated by the sarcophagi. Get him to lift the lid on the bigger of the two. Point out some flaw inside, right at the top, where the head rests. He would bend over. She'd lift the sock, weighted with the ingots, high over her shoulder, then bring it down, sharply. And fatally. Conveniently, he would fall into the gaping hole, lengthwise. Then, firmly, she'd close the lid and secure it. Lock the door between the two rooms. Deposit the key in its usual place, under the delicately modelled foot of a statue of the goddess Kali, for safe keeping. Back with the ingots on the shelf, and a pair of men's socks for the wash. She had vowed never to wash a man's socks. But sometimes notions of right and wrong demand flexibility. The exception proves the rule, she thought, and anyway, one couldn't donate, albeit anonymously through the large St Vincent's box standing like a mail receptacle on the post office steps, dirty socks to the poor.

He was due back today, at 4.15 PM. She would take him into the storeroom as soon as he arrived, just to clarify his intentions about those sarcophagi. Would they stay, or would they go? Just as well there was nothing else to put in the space, if he had decided to hang onto them hoping for the return of the Gold.

"Ms Hamilton? Mr Hamilton had to rush off again. The Congolese art exhibition at the New South Wales Gallery is ending tonight, so he landed at Tullamarine at 4.15 pm, came straight to the office from the airport, then said he had to go off for the Sydney showing." She took a quick breath, then went on. "He got me to fix him up for West Africa, flying out of Sydney tomorrow. He'll phone if he can from the hotel tonight, or if it's too late, tomorrow from the airport. But he said you'd understand if he couldn't get to the telephone.

"The next fashion is in African art, he says, and with the numbers going to the African candidate for Commonwealth Secretary General, it confirms the trend. May be a longshot, but he's taking it for the sake of the business."

"Don't want to end up with trunks full of spears and heads or assegai like the sarcophagi? No, no, Ms Hamilton. I don't think there'll be anything joining the sarcophagi now for a time. They're taking up room there, but they're in safekeeping.

"What about the gasworks down the back of the plant...We could have it renovated, and add in an airtight storage space. We'll likely have the sarcophagi on our hands for some time, so with another space we wouldn't have to disturb them. Don't like to touch them without his say-so. Mr Hamilton can decide when they're to go. I did ask him today...listened, but he didn't seem to have much to say. Africa on his mind, I expect."

"No, didn't say when he'd be heading back. A long trip through Africa. Namibia, Zimbabwe, Kenya, all down the coast. He's got an open 'round the world' ticket. And American Express is all paid up."

"West and East, I think. Perhaps Madagascar...And he was talking about South America sometime ago too."

"Mentioned Bolivia and Chile to you too, did he, Ms Hamilton...the Andes...Straight on from Africa to South America? Oh, dear, Ms Hamilton, will you be able to cope with the house and the children with him being away all that time?"

"Yes, fine, Ms Hamilton, when he rings in again I'll let you know...You might drop by later in the week...Fine...Bye."

"Ms Hamilton, could you drop by the office some time, perhaps tomorrow or Wednesday? Just some documents to sign. The gasworks conversion. Architect's plans are looking good. I think Mr Hamilton would approve.

"Yes, when he gets back from New Guinea it'll be a really pleasant surprise. No, don't think he's anywhere near Bourgainville."

"I'm not sure. He did mention, some time ago, something about Rhodes. And a hankering to go back to Egypt...No, no, *no* repeat of the sarcophagi. He seemed to take it to heart last time I mentioned them. I don't think we need fear any more landing on the storeroom vestibule, even if he does go on to Egypt from Bali...Yes, some more batik...steady seller, it is..."

"Ms Hamilton? I'm a little concerned about the business. There's more in this office than one person can handle. Time we expanded into a two person office, perhaps even another 'front person'."

"Yes, there's so much business to be done on the overseas side. I don't think Mr Hamilton can keep up with it. We have to renew our contacts in Japan. With the new gasworks as an exhibition hall, we can expand...

"Yes, I always have my passport at the ready Ms Hamilton."

"Oh, you'll pop by today to look in? Fine."

"Ms Fountain, *I* will join you in the business. I've been the 'silent partner' too long. After-school care's already organised for the children. I can be in here from 8.30 AM to 5.30 PM every day, or however late we have to stay for getting exhibitions together.

"The children and I've had a marvellous time with the microwave. All those big roasts I was doing aren't really necessary. Roger was – is so fond of roasts that we'd got into a bit of a habit.

"We've taken to going to MacDonald's Friday nights for a treat. A treat for them and a break for me. Even Tom at fifteen is young enough to be impressed with a 'Big Mac' and french fries every week. To him, it's decadence plus!"

"No, no the children are quite all right. I'm keeping them up with their father's trip. They're really more interested in the Saturday soccer, to tell you the truth, and as long as I'm there to be the chauffeur, they're perfectly happy. He's been away most of their lives. Dashing in on the odd occasion, then off for another buying trip. The school got quite used to seeing only me on prize nights years ago, or 'discussions with the class teacher'. 'Parent involvement', I think they call it. But then, I'm just the typical parent. Most of us are single mothers at those events, whether divorced or separated or just married as Roger − Mr Hamilton − and I. With Roger away like this, nothing has really changed, you see. Except it's MacDonald's and the microwave. And I've been moving the rooms around a bit.

"I'm sure Roger will love it when he comes back. He never did use the study, so all my books are in there, now, and out of the diningroom. Thought I could start writing an art column, from the study as it were. *Artsabroad* may take my stuff."

"You know it? Attend the Art Collective meetings? Yes, certainly, I'll go along for you while you're away. High time I got myself involved in something out of the house. The children can babysit themselves nowadays on the odd occasion. Builds up self-reliance."

"Yes, it's good to get your weekly messages from him, that his trip's going smoothly. But − you've planned your Japan trip, haven't you, now he's off in Iceland? The Japanese may be interested in our Aboriginal art. You'll handle all that eastern charm so well."

"Trouble keeping the office going while you're away? No, no, don't you worry about a thing. I've picked up a lot from these telephone discussions we've been having lately, or popping in. I never did talk much with Roger about it – Mr Hamilton – but every time he was away – away, before – I kept up with the background, just through your calls to me with his messages from abroad, or interstate…And that's another thing. There have been no interstate trips since he's been away this time. We can't let our Sydney and Perth contacts get away from us. And there's the Broome leg now, and Daly River, and Katherine, what with the boom in Aboriginal art."

"Yes, Ms Fountain, you take all responsibility for the overseas contacts. I'll 'hold the shop', make sure the exhibition goes well. By the time you're back, we'll have more orders than we can handle for 'Art from Tennant Creek'. Then I'll do the interstaters, and you can hold shop. I haven't been to Perth since 1964 when Roger and I were on our honeymoon. I'll zip up to the Ord, then down to Esperance. Up to Kalgoorlie and Boulder. We can run another exhibition. Fly someone over to open it."

"Yes, Ms Fountain…Look, do call me Beth…You're Margaret? Yes, Margaret, well do have a great trip o/s…I've got your itinerary here, and you'll call in regularly. Don't do anything I wouldn't do.

"Yes, I'll take very great care of the art works, and the office, and the plant…Oh, and that's the key to the office storeroom…Thanks. Just as well to know where it is. It's kept safely under the foot of Kali, I see. And we keep the money and small valuables in front section…And the sarcophagi are in the back? No need to disturb them, I certainly agree. No, I have no desire to emulate Nefertiti, nor the beautiful Helen…I've had quite sufficient in the Egyptology line to last me for quite some time, and I dare say you have too, Margaret. Don't want to unleash the wrath of Tutankhamen at this time of life. No, I dare say they're good and airtight in that storage space, no point in disturbing the sleep of the Pharaohs."

On the Land

Mrs Snook stood back and surveyed her handiwork. With a sigh of satisfaction she let her eyes wander slowly over the trays set out in smart rows before her. Trays piled high with doorstop sandwiches, the slices of bread an inch thick. Sandwiches with good, solid fillings. Fat slabs of roast beef with tomato sauce. Not that commercial kind, in the bird-bedecked bottles. Home made, here in Bundajarra, by Mrs Snook herself. She harvested the tomatoes from her own garden, scores of them, every season. Spent days in the large kitchen slicing, pickling, potting. Mixed in the finely sliced onions, the mint and, in some jars – just to give it that extra tang – nasturtium leaves.

There were sandwiches with thick pink slivers of ham poking out, ham liberally spread with hot, homemade mustard pickle. In others, large, succulent pieces of tomato with shiny skin showed between the slices of brown, homemade bread. White bread and sausage sandwiches. Perhaps not so wholesome. But a real favourite amongst the men in the AFF, the Association of Fighting Farmers, a new group started up in Bundajarra in these times of economic crisis (as the men saw it), and essential to the survival of *our* way of life.

She glanced over at Mrs Curtis. Mrs Curtis was putting the last liberal scoop of butter on the last hot scone. Plunging a large ladle into a tub of homemade raspberry jam, she gouged out a generous mound, spreading it with care on to the scone so that it ran in warm red rivulets down the crispy sides and melted into the creamy soft texture of the centre. "There," she said, almost to herself in obvious delight. "That's done for another week." She looked at Mrs Snook and met her eyes. "They won't find fault with any of this, not that it's even remotely possible, Jean."

Mrs Longyear joined them from the end of the counter, walking up slowly along the trays of sandwiches, the plates piled high with scones. She had been fixing the cake, cutting large chunks off the cherry and raisin filled slabs baked in her own ovens, and those of Mrs Barratt-Lennard. Mrs Barratt-Lennard, meanwhile, stood together with Mrs Fleay at the stove, which spread over almost the entire wall of the kitchen of the civic centre. Their task was complete. The pots of soup bubbled gently, simmering over the hotplates. Peas bounced about alongside succulent pieces of ham, chasing each other around the hockbone which slowly rose and fell in a steady rhythm. Rounds of carrots and parsnip ran at each other, round and around the smooth sides of a shining saucepan, pushing themselves against the bits of beef and lamb that bobbed up and down, fighting for space. Cauliflower and leek coated themselves in a creamy smooth, saucey concoction of parsley and cheese.

"Let the AFF come to order," intoned Barry Barratt-Lennard in his usual deep voice. "There's a long list of business to be got through this afternoon. We've got resolutions on the deregulation of the wheat industry, doing away with the Wheat Board as they are – well, if we let them get away with it. Then there's the fight we're having with the local shire about the sealing of Daveys Road. And there's that pig farm that's been started up down the valley. It could be ruinous if those small farmers start coming into the area. We've got to take a stand, find out who's behind it and run them out of town on a rail." He banged the table with a gavel, specially bought for such occasions. "Now," he said, turning around to look at the door behind him. "Where are the ladies?"

Just as he spoke, the door opened, revealing Mrs Snook and Mrs Fleay standing solidly at the sides of a large chrome trolley. Firmly and surely they pushed it into the room, the aromas of hot peas and ham, beef and lamb and tomatoes and cheese and leek and carrots and parsnip wafting before them. On the next shelf down, deep baskets of crisp, brown buttered rolls jostled for space. With an efficiency born of long days working as "the ladies" of the Rural Women's Society, serving lunches and dinners and breakfasts and teas to every men's organisation that ever existed in Bundajarra and surrounds, every soup bowl standing before every member of the AFF was filled to the brim with the soup of his choice. Rolls were laid out, two to a side plate. Mrs Longyear and Mrs Curtis followed along beside the trolley, which was manoeuvred over the slightly ridged floor of the civic centre by Mrs Snook and Mrs Fleay. The women worked in tandem, Mrs Longyear and Mrs Curtis ladling the soup, after gently and unobtrusively enquiring of the men which they preferred.

It didn't make much difference: all wanted each soup; all that changed was the order of their drinking them, from time to time. Except for Mr Curtis, whom all the women knew was partial to Mrs Fleay's pea and ham. For him, three large helpings of the Fleay speciality.

Mrs Snook and Mrs Fleay pushed the trolley and, between times, scooped out the bread rolls from the lower shelf. Then, appearing from the kitchen, Mrs Barratt-Lennard came up at the rear, hovering just behind as the trolley-parade progressed, keeping a friendly but efficient eye on the serious business of serving the food.

Round and around the table went Mrs Snook and Mrs Fleay, together with Mrs Curtis and Mrs Longyear, followed by Mrs Barratt-Lennard. And all the time the men, in between bites of roll and spoonings of soup, talked their way through the agenda. "It's either get more representation on to the Shire, or give up on Daveys Road altogether," said Mr Curtis. "They're never going to seal it. All the land we've bought up along it is absolutely useless. It's time we cut our losses. What d'you reckon, Bob?" "Well," said Bob Snook. "I reckon you're just about right, Andy. But who's going to be fool enough to buy parcels and parcels of country without any proper access road, I ask you. Okay for the days of the drays, horse and buggy days, but the 1990s? Not on your nelly. Can't get trucks in, can't get trucks out. Tractors bogged in winter. Broken down in summer. Dust and dirt and gravel in your eyes. No..."

"You're right Bob," chimed in Dave Longyear. "But we've got to try. I vote we put it on the market right now. An ad in the *Farmers' Advertiser*...and what about the *Westralian*? Might catch some of those St George's Terrace farmers, waddaya reckon?"

"Right. Okay. That's the way we go, fellas," boomed Barry Barratt-Lennard. "But I say we advertise in the East, too. What about an ad in those eastern papers – the *Age*, the *Sydney Morning Herald*. Maybe its more likely we'll catch the Pitt Street farmers or the Collins Street mob that way. They might come in suckers."

By this time, the soups had been drunk, bread rolls were a memory, apart from the few crumbs that littered table and floor. All around Mr Curtis' feet, noticed Mrs Longyear, were signs of his ravenous eating habits. She glanced at Ruth. Ruth Curtis looked back, and raised her eyebrows.

The trolley disappeared back into the kitchen. The men went on to the next item on the agenda, the pig farm. Like a flash, the trolley was back, Mrs Barratt-Lennard at one side this time, opposite Mrs Curtis. Trayloads of sandwiches filled both shelves. Round and around went Mrs Barratt-Lennard, Mrs Curtis, and the trolley. Round and around went Mrs Snook and Mrs Fleay, serving the sandwiches, with gentle, murmuring voices requesting of the men of the AFF their choice of ham, sausage, tomato, beef...Generally, it was ham, sausage, tomato and beef, the women remarked. Oh, not in loud voices, nor in soft voices, but in the locking of eyes over the heads of these men, the leading lights of Bundajarra. The farming fraternity that dreamt of running the town. Back to the days when there were no interlopers, the townsmen, members of Rotary, members of the Shire Council who weren't "on the land". The carpetbaggers of the West. Up at the rear, Mrs Longyear kept her eyes open, at every moment aware of which of the men had finished whatever he had on his plate. Which had to be served next, even if it was out of turn. Mrs Longyear had an overall view of the table. Her eyes picked up everything. Sometimes, as she glanced down and saw how much one man was eating, how he was stuffing the sandwiches (two at a time, often) into his gaping mouth, she looked up, her eyes meeting those of Mrs Snook. Or Mrs Curtis. Or Mrs Fleay. Or Mrs Barratt-Lennard.

"Yes, the pig farm," grumbled Mr Longyear. Mrs Longyear happened to be standing right behind him as he said it, and she kept her eyes calmly focused on the empty plate beside his fat, hairy fist, until it was safe to look up. She walked softly over to the trolley, which by that time had come to rest at Mr Curtis' elbow, and took up several sandwiches on a spare plate. Back she went to deposit them at Mr Longyear's side. "I think," he was going on, "We've just got to get to the bottom of it. Who actually owns it, that's what I want to know. Those people down there. Couldn't even call them women. How can they run the thing? They'll be out on their ear before long, I'm telling you now. Go bankrupt if it is theirs, or drive the real owners bankrupt, anyway. But before they do, what're the chances the whole place will go to rack and ruin, if the knowledge gets about that there's pig farmers moving into Bundajarra territory?"

"I agree, Dave." Mr Fleay spoke up, this time, obviously angry and upset. His face was red. He was stuttering and spluttering, bits of sausage spurting out of his thick lips on to the tablecloth.

Mrs Snook watched, silent. Have to put the dogs on first, to lick it clean before the wash, this time, she thought, looking at the ruin of the sheet they used to cover the wooden trestles. Her eyes met Mrs Fleay's.

"What's say we get Bungle, Broadhurst and Mash to look into it," said Mr Barratt-Lennard firmly. "Steve Mash is a townie, but he's okay if you want to get legal work done. He can do a search and we can see what he comes up with, then we move on from there."

There were general mutterings of agreement. Tony Fleay's cheeks went back to their normal colour and he managed to keep firm hold of the ham and pickle sandwich he held in his left hand, whilst with his right, he slapped Barratt-Lennard on the back. "Good on you, mate. We'll get those pigs and women out of this town before sundown."

The kitchen door slid gently to a close behind the trolley. Mrs Curtis and Mrs Snook remained behind, with the men, to clear the dinner plates, which they had used for the sandwiches, from the table and replace them with fresh bread and butter plates. It was time for the cakes.

Out sailed the trolley, on its last but one excursion into the civic centre diningroom for this Tuesday Association of Fighting Farmers meeting. Mrs Fleay and Mrs Barratt-Lennard pushed it into the room, plates of cake and scones piled high. Mrs Longyear plied the men with first this plate, then the next. The food came unobtrusively into the men's grasp. They didn't even notice the thick slices of cake appearing at each one's left hand, their plates being piled with scones dripping with butter and jam, so intent were they on the horrors wreaked upon them by a Canberra socialist government. Deregulation of the wheat market. Abolition of the Wheat Board. An end to the world-as-we-know-it. Yet somehow, in the midst of the furious debate, the voices rising louder and louder, the faces growing brighter and brighter, Mr Fleay's face almost burning with the measure of his rage – each and every one, their hands sought and found the cake and the scones; their hands lifted the cake and the scones mouthwards; their mouths devoured.

The trolley was back, now, for its final round of the table. Strong cups of tea were poured and drunk. The Tuesday meeting was over. The farmers went back to their farms. The women (farmers too, they at least knew, but with an added task today) cleared the plates and cups, washed, scoured the pots and pans, wiped down the surfaces of stove, trolley and counter. And, finally, locked up. And while they cleared and washed and scoured and wiped, they talked. Their talk was of pig farms and sealing of roads, too. But the content was different from that of the talk of Tony Fleay, and Mr Longyear, and Andy Curtis, and Mr Barratt-Lennard, and Bob Snook. And the conclusions, too.

The councillors of the Shire met Thursdays at noon. They sent out their agendas beforehand, circulated together with backup papers, typed by the steno-secs in the Shire offices, down the street from the civic centre. The steno-secs did not, of course, attend the Shire meetings. This was the one occasion that the word "secretary" was attached to a man, and a man actually took notes. Bernie Fitzgibbon, Shire secretary, took pride in his work. And so he should. He was paid an honorarium of $28,000 a year, for attending two meetings each month and handing on his handwritten note pad to Suzy James down at the Shire offices, who was paid $17,700 a year for her full-time secretarial services. Among other tasks, to her it fell to decipher the writing and produce "Minutes of the Shire Meeting" the day after, to be circulated for confirmation the following fortnight.

At the civic centre, the good ladies of the Rural Women's Society, more often known as the RWS, had spent the morning preparing for the men. Again, the soups and sauces bubbling on the stove. Again, the trays piled high with roundly filled sandwiches, sitting solidly upon the counter ready for the trolley. Again, the plates filled with cakes and scones jostling for position, awaiting eagerly their transfer to trolley, table, mouths of the men. Messrs Snook, Curtis, Barratt-Lennard, Fleay and Longyear surveyed the kitchen, their domain. They were ready.

"Daveys Road down there at Bundajarra," said Irwin Leonard, Shire councillor. "That farming lot have been on about the sealing for God knows how long. Much as I hate to say it though, they do have a point. Not good for the Shire to have it lying potholed in summer, what with the dust and the heat, then waterlogged in winter. It's not only their cars that get bogged you know. I got bogged one day last year and it was nearly bloody murder before I got out. Didn't ever let on to anyone, at the time, because we would have looked right jackasses if I got bogged, then we sealed her. But I vote we get in the council workers, set them to it, and have done with it."

Mrs Snook carefully ladled the cheese, leak and chicken soup into Councillor Leonard's bowl. He took up his spoon and slurped the steaming liquid into his open mouth. Next to him, Mr Fitzgibbon was slurping happily too. His first choice today was the beef and vegetable. Delicious. Further down the table, where Mrs Barratt-Lennard was ladling out the lamb and tomato, Councillor Andrews took the opportunity opened by Councillor Leonard's pause, jumping in to agree. "Yes, no doubt about it. I vote we seal Daveys Road and have done with it. I'm sick of all the lobbying that lot are doing. Bloody farmers. Think they own the place. Setting up the AFF. I'll give them "Fighting Farmers". If it's not the day it's the night. All hours on the telephone. Bailed up in the street. When can a man get about his lawful business, I ask you. You've got my vote."

Heads nodded in agreement. Mrs Longyear looked carefully around the table, noting the brimming plates, the crusty bread rolls secure at each man's left hand. Just in passing, her eyes lighted upon the nodding heads. Heads bobbing in unison. Ah, she thought. The men have made a decision. Casually she glanced over at Mrs Snook and Mrs Curtis who just happened to be standing beside Mr Fitzgibbon at that moment. Mr Fitzgibbon was writing rapidly in his notebook, as if he wanted to get the words down as soon as possible to ratify the vote. And to free his hands to begin on his next choice of soup, the beef, barley and vegetable. The Snook, Curtis and Longyear eyes met. And even with their backs slightly turned to the table, as Mrs Fleay and Mrs Barratt-Leonard began to move the trolley out, back towards the kitchen, it was almost as if they had a sixth sense: they knew with a certainty that the heads were nodding, heard the pen scratching on Mr Fitzgibbon's notebook. They knew the time had come to make that immediate contact with Phenella Fortesque of Fortesque, Martin and Blanchard, Solicitors (an all woman firm newly established in Northam, just 60 kilometres west). Phenella was waiting for the call. The paperwork was already done. The advertisements responded to. The offers ready to be taken up, accepted, signed on the dotted line. It was time to move. Mrs Snook quickly made her way out of the civic centre to the carpark and slipped unobtrusively into the public telephone box located conveniently on the corner, where she could not possibly be overheard. "Reverse charges, please, to Phenella Fortesque of Fortesque, Martin and Blanchard, thank you. It's a Northam number, 608 4445," she said crisply.

Back at the civic centre, the trolley laden with sandwiches had already passed through the door between kitchen and diningroom. Ham, beef, lamb, tomato, wholemeal bread, brown bread, white bread, sausages, tongue, all were being devoured between grunts of masculine pleasure. Another major problem of the Shire solved. And all in one afternoon. The satisfaction of men well pleased by a decision swelled out, catching her as she eased through the door to take her place at the trolley. Mrs Longyear, Mrs Curtis, Mrs Fleay and Mrs Barratt-Lennard saw Mrs Snook's head bow slightly toward them, a sign between women of a decision well-made and rapidly executed.

The rest of the day went quickly. Pikelets with jam and cream. Rich, dark fruitcake, moist and inviting on the plates. The men sensed it was "hometime". They had made a decision. No point in lingering. But they stayed, anyway, to finish the last crumbs of cake, washed down with the dregs of tea from the freshly brewed pots. In the kitchen, the washing and drying and wiping and cleaning went briskly, efficiently, like the clockwork of the women's households.

On Fridays, the RWS "did" lunch for the businessmen of Bundajarra, the men of the local Rotary Club. This was the club of the despised "townies" the Association of Fighting Farmers moaned about during their AFF meetings on Tuesdays. But Bundajarra was Bundajarra. Rotary Club lunches (meetings, that is, with the serious conduct of business) were held at the civic centre. The Rural Women's Society simmered soups, buttered bread, cut doorstop sandwiches, baked bread and breadrolls, sliced cake, whipped cream, and did all those things they did best, just as they did them for the meetings of the Shire and for the AFF.

Today, it was minestrone, and onion and leak soup, and a thick, creamy soup of mixed beans, pork and tomato. In place of the traditional sandwiches there was pizza. Pizza with ham and chives and anchovies. Pizza with tomato, bacon and mozzarella. Pizza with capsicum, sausage, and a fine sprinkling of parmesan stirred briskly with chopped bacon. Rotary, after all, had a membership slightly more adventurous than the AFF and the Shire. And who knew, it may well pay to introduce some more exotic dishes into the Tuesday and Thursday lunches. Mrs Snook, Mrs Curtis and Mrs Barratt-Lennard saw there was every enthusiasm amongst the Rotary members for pizza. Would the AFF and the Shire like it, sometimes, too?

As the cheeses were being passed around with the home-made crackers and bread baked rusk-like in the oven, Steve Mash of Bungle, Broadhurst and Mash, Bundajarra's sole firm of solicitors, spoke up. "That pig farm down there by the intersection of Daveys Road and the Great Eastern Highway. Run by a couple of women. Hairy-legged feminists I think you'd call them. The AFF – Barry Barratt-Lennard – has been on to me to get rid of them. Find out who's behind it. Can't believe those women could actually own it. Well, you know, he's right. There's something behind it all, that's for sure. But I can't get a lead on it from anywhere. Done a title search. All in order. No faults or muckups. But somewhere, something smells." He took a large bite of blue vein smeared in large globules on a man-sized rusk. "Can't get to the bottom of it. Nothing on them. Can't get them out. Barry's not going to like it, I can tell you. Those Fighting Farmers are fighting, but I can't see them getting anywhere on that issue real fast. All above board. I might think it's a mystery. How that land was bought up from old MacKenzie so quickly that it seemed someone in the AFF must have leaked it somewhere that he was selling up. Or even that one of that mob, one of the Fighters themselves might have stolen the lead on the others. But no. There's something there. How those women knew about it and grabbed it up. Why it seems that there's a company landlord somewhere in the background. The whole thing smells, I don't know why. But I do know that they're not going to be able to get rid of them easily. If at all. I reckon those women – and the pigs – are here to stay. And I'll tell you something else. I reckon there's something going on with all that land down around Daveys Road. I reckon it's connected. There's some massive company take-over pending on the land around here, that's all I can tell you. No evidence. No concrete evidence. I just feel it in my bones." He put a piece of Jarlsberg, as big as the two first fingers of his right hand, into his mouth, following it rapidly with a couple of crackers that crunched between his jaws. "I just know it. There'll be more women in there, running more pigs, or worse, before you can turn around." He took up the cup of steaming coffee that had appeared, silently and as if by an invisible hand, at his elbow. "I promise you," he said, nodding sagely around the table. "There'll be more for the AFF to fight about than the Wheat Board. Pigs and women. Pigs and women. They won't get them off the agenda in a hurry."

Tuesday. The AFF was meeting as usual at the Bundajarra civic centre. There was pea and ham soup on the menu. Pork and potato, and onion with gloriously yellow, thick, creamily melting strands of cheese arrayed on golden croutons of home-made bread. The AFF had taken to pizza, wolfing down the servings with gusto. They were taken with the hugh chunks of cheese and biscuits, followed by something sweet. Cake and pikelets, scones with honey and jam and cream stood poised on the trolleys at the hands of the RWS.

Talk turned to the land around Daveys Road.

"We sure got done in on that one," said Tony Fleay, going his usual red in the face. "Sold the land. Thought we all got a good deal. Thought we'd foxed some limey from the Eastern States. Got ourselves out of a rotten land deal, so we thought. And look at it now. Someone making money out of that land at last. Sealed road. Newest road in town, in fact. Some new process. Last longer than any other road in the shire, so they say."

"It's almost as if someone was spying on us," said Barry Barrett-Lennard. "Seems that someone knew almost before we did that we'd decided to throw in the towel and sell that land."

Dave Longyear nodded. "Yes, but we never let anyone into our AFF meetings," he said. "Never anyone here but us. And it couldn't be one of us, could it?" The others looked at him.

"But we've all been done in, over this," they exclaimed at once.

"Every one of us," went on Bob Snook. "Trapped by some Collins Street or Pitt Street farmer. Or even one of our own, some know-it-all, know nothing from Perth. St George's Terrace farmers. They're probably the worst kind. Doing us out of our rights. That's our land they've got."

"Still," chipped in Andy Curtis. "At least they haven't put more pigs in, yet. More of those hairy-legged women, yes. But pigs, no. Cows, I think I saw there the other day. No beef cattle though. The whole countryside's going namby pamby, that's the problem. No real guts anymore. Pigs and cows. I ask you."

Out in the kitchen, at the end of the day, the wiping and the washing went on as usual. Mrs Snook, Mrs Curtis, Mrs Longyear, Mrs Barratt-Lennard and Mrs Fleay companionably continued their work. Tonight was the regular monthly meeting of the Rural Women's Society. The RWS had been good to them. Tonight, they were holding a joint meeting of the RWS and the Bundajarra Women's Collective. They had decided to turn one of the large blocks on Daveys Road over to pig farming, to complement their earlier venture, and were to decide the process of interview for the women shortlisted from the many applicants to run it. The other blocks were to be devoted to cows. What with milking and making cheeses, there was a real future in getting the land run competently. And making a comfortable profit. All without resorting to the exploitative techniques of "modern" farming. Their expertise, built up on their own farms would be useful; it would be built on. There was obviously a market in Bundajarra for cheeses. Why eat imported Jarlsberg when you could eat, and sell, Bundajarra Gold. And what about Bundajarra Blue? The possibilities were endless.

Mrs Snook gave the sink a last brisk whisk. Mrs Curtis made sure the oven was turned off, and gave a final polish to the brass knobs over the range. Mrs Barratt-Lennard stacked the trays and plates, sorting the civic centre crockery from hers and Mrs Longyear's. Mrs Longyear took up her pile, after sweeping the top of the counter with a dishcloth. Mrs Fleay flicked at the trolley with a teatowel. Out they went, turning off the lights and shutting the door behind them. Mrs Curtis turned the key in the lock and handed it to Mrs Snook. Mrs Snook, taller than the others, reached up and put it in its "secret" place (the whole town knew, really) between the wall and the architrave of the main entrance hall door. They were looking forward to tonight's RWS meeting.

Cleaning – or Cleaning Up

LUISA BEZZINA SCRUBBED hard at the white porcelain of the toilet bowl, then sat back on her heels, panting slightly. Pausing for only a moment, she wiped one hand quickly across her forehead. Then it was back, head down, elbows up, scrubbing so that the bowl shone.

On the other side of the floor, Penelope Cugliari pressed down firmly on the vacuum cleaner as she pushed it along the carpet. She, too, paused momentarily, then went on, leaning forward as she moved over the springy surface, towards the open doors of the offices.

On the floor below, Angelina Abelardo squirted Mr Sheen on the glass table tops near the comfortable chairs that stood, waiting for the morning and the clients who sat, patiently, idly turning the pages of *Fortune,* or *Business Review Weekly* and *Australian Business.* Polishing with a vigour born of long experience in cleaning offices, she was startled by a voice coming from behind her, near the desk that stood between her and the offices she had just finished vacuuming. "Angelina, watch out. He's coming," Gena Boccassini mouthed at her. She flicked the cloth in her hands and polished harder.

"Okay, Angelina, get moving…I know, I know. No complaints from this floor, or the one above, for that matter. That's true. But no need to fall down on the job. No resting. Got to get the lot finished on time. No slacking."

It was Radivoj Cayhan, the boss. He was doing his usual prowl, around the offices, up and down the inner staircases, seeing who was working and who was not. Who was working hard, and who was breathing on the job. Breathing was out!

Vacuuming, scrubbing, dusting, polishing, shining, scouring – were *in*. And no breathers in between. No sitting down, no resting, no leaning up against the broom for a minute. Even a second.

Radivoj Cayhan had his workforce well trained. For the first half hour, from 7.00 PM until 7.30, he walked around, checking up on the cleaners, making sure that they were at work, not sitting down somewhere, having a smoko. The way he arranged his visits, they never knew when he might come upon them. It was good that way, he thought. "Keep 'em on their toes."

For the next three hours, give or take half an hour, he would settle himself in the executive staffroom at the top of the building, fifty-four floors up, gazing down on the Harbour. There, he turned on the widescreen television set, poured himself a scotch, or a bourbon (depending on his mood and the contents of the executive liquor cabinet), and stretched out. He saw the games shows, or the late news and the current affairs programmes that followed, then some soapy, or a foreign language film (as they called them) on SBS, or an ABC special.

Then, for the last half hour, up to 11.00 PM, it was back on the prowl again. Popping up here and there when they least expected it. Checking on the smooth surfaces in the boardroom and offices; looking into the lavatories at random, inspecting the stainless steel of the urinals and taps, the ceramic sinks and bowls, pulling open the paper towel holders at random, making sure they were sufficiently full, but not so full the sheets wouldn't drop easily to the aperture at the bottom. Sometimes, he picked up papers and books that lay at random on desks and chairs and sidetables, just checking to see that the duster had not passed them by, leaving clean, oblong shapes underneath, surrounded by a dull grey mist.

He had never caught them out, not the four who did from the fiftieth floor through to the fifty-fourth. Sometimes, he had had to sack one of the women on the floors below. Or give them a good talking to, warning them that their jobs were on the line. Once, he had had to get rid of three of them, for ignoring the need for some old-fashioned elbow grease.

Melissa Chan

He had picked up these anglo-isms from Sammy May, the contract cleaner who had given him his supervisor's job in the high AMP Building, overlooking the Quay. Sammy May now ran the business from his home in Wahroonga, up the North Shore line. His way of checking was to ring through to Radivoj now and then, using the line in the executive suite. Sammy May knew how it worked. Who worked. How they worked. That supervising was an art. And he knew he had a good supervisor in Radivoj Cayhan. No complaints from the AMP Building. Never. Not now.

No, thought Radivoj, leaning back with his arms above his head, folded across the top of the large lounge chair as he sat watching the titles bursting on to the screen, advertising the coming newscast. "It's going along fine."

At that moment there was a timid knock on the door. Luisa Bezzina shyly put her head around the door. "Everything okay, Luisa?" asked Radivoj. "Yes, yes," said Luisa hastily. "I was wondering...I was wondering if you had everything you need...Actually, I brought in some scallopini – homemade – thought you might like it." She came into the room, bearing a large dish covered with a red and white chequered cloth. Radivoj Cayhan's nostrils twitched, as they did every weekday evening, whether it was Luisa and her speciality, or Angelina and steaming dishes of eggs or omlettes, cooked with herbs and cream, or Penelope and crispy potatoes and chopped bacon sprinkled with tangy spices and scented herbs, or Gena and her spaghetti bolognaise or marinara, the fine threads of spaghetti smothered in sumptuous sauces. "Great women, these," he thought, his chest expanding with good will, his stomach rumbling as it confidently prepared itself, making room for Luisa's cooking.

Luisa placed the bowl on the sidetable, near Radivoj's right side, unwrapping a fork and spoon from a large white napkin she had been balancing underneath. "Enjoy!" she said, bowing her head slightly, as she silently left the room, her feet hardly touching the floor. Picking up fork and spoon, Radivoj Cayhan began to eat.

It all began when Gena Boccassini joined the cleaners assigned to the top floors of the AMP Building. Somehow, she brought the trio – now four – luck. The week she joined, they had put in their Lotto form as usual. The only difference was that Gena was the fourth contributor, the fourth member of the syndicate.

She had worked for three years at the Sydney Stock Exchange, down on Bond Street, running the vacuum cleaner over the floors, picking up the slips of paper that seemed to swamp every office in the building, and particularly the floor of the Exchange, down where the buying and selling of stocks and shares went on. But she had had a falling out with the boss, Mr Armenio.

Peter Armenio was a hard taskmaster. Gena Boccassini was a good worker. But she made him uncomfortable. He had come upon her on one occasion in the library, reading. Reading when she was supposed to be wiping down the table tops. And what she was reading. Not just the *Daily Mirror* or the *Sun,* before it went out of business. Not even the *Sun Herald.* But the *Financial Review*! What was she thinking about, he exclaimed to himself as he pounced on her, almost tearing the flimsy pages from her hands. "What are you doing here, woman," he shouted at her, as he flung the newspaper back on the rack.

"It's cleaning for you. Cleaning. No lazing about reading. Reading! And this – this – Think you're working in the Stock Exchange, do you? You're working at cleaning, Gena Boccassini, and don't you ever forget that. Clean. Clean. Clean!"

His voice bellowed out, over the silent racks of papers – *Asian Wall Street Journal,* the *New York Times, Australian Financial Review* – and the business magazines. She had taken up the feather duster that lay on one of the large tables used by readers during the day, and with an outward calm flicked at the rows of books packing the shelves. Her heart was beating faster, involuntarily alarmed at the noise.

The next time he caught her in the library, Peter Armenio demoted her. It was worse this time. She was reading a book. *How to Chart Your Way to Success on the Share Market*, by Merril Armstrong. Reading a newspaper was bad enough. But a *book*. On *shares*. On *buying* and *selling* and SUCCESS!

"Out, out, out," he shouted. And it was out to the Exchange floor, to clean the writing from the black boards, to suck up in a large vacuum cleaner the chalk dust which fell on the ledges and benches, the tables and partitions. The dust which made her cough, choking as the clouds billowed around her feet, rising up to engulf her chin and eyes and hair, with the motion of the vacuum and the duster as she poked at the layers of fine chalk resting on every available surface. The chalk dust which rose and darkened and smeared the glass area at the top, where people looked down from the public gallery.

Sometimes Gena Boccassini arrived early to watch the Exchange in operation, the times between 10.00 AM and 1.00 PM, and 2.00 PM to 4.00, when the chalkies stood high on a ledge above the floor, writing up figures on the boards, rubbing them off and replacing them as the calls came through. She had watched the men in their striped shirts (and a few, so few, women), walking purposefully about the floor below. There was a style of dress on the floor of the Exchange, she noted, counting four men in red striped, white shirts, six in shirts with broad white bands between dark stripes. Pale blue, and green, and grey shirts mingled. And several of pale blue, with thin, red stripes...She worked out, for herself, the system: the buying broker's number appeared in one column. Next to it appeared the bid. In the next column was the offer. And in the fourth column was written the selling broker's number. In another column the chalkies, standing high above the crowd, wrote the highest price paid for the shares, over a line under which they wrote the lowest price paid for the shares. And in the last column, the last sale was written. Overhead, the Translux, the old ticker tape now projected through a computer system, recorded the names of the companies and their shares, the price at which the shares were sold, and the number of shares sold. And it recorded, in lighted squares, the latest movements on the market: whether sales in various industries were up or down, whether values of shares in the industries were booming – or busting. It ran continuously, the illuminated figures and letters chasing each other along the top of the boards. "Gold Down. Engineering Up. Paper Prod. Down. WLZ. EMLZ. Other Metals Down. Oil Gas Down. All Rev. Down.

Develop. Contract Up. Building Mat. Down." Below, on the boards, the names of companies trading on the market appeared, in lists, one above the other: "ANZ. BHP. ACMEX. Adsteam. Advance. BTR Nylex. Çoles Myer. Elders IXL. Fletcher/Goodman. Ind. Equity. Lend Lease. News Corp. TNT. Westpac. Faulding." Gena sat in the gallery, mesmerised. Engrossed. Taking it all in.

Her last day was cataclysmic. Mr Armenio discovered she had, that afternoon, attended an information session on how the Stock Exchange works. Just a public relations exercise run by the Exchange, for school children, university and college students, the general public. Gena Boccassini had attended under the heading "general public". She had just as much right to be there as anyone. But not according to Peter Armenio.

She had listened intently to the short introductory background of trading in stocks and shares, the brief history of stockbroking recounted by the man from the public relations office who ran the session. How the British system began in the coffee houses in London, where the brokers ran raffles and lotteries when selling was slow. They were thrown out in 1642 from their possey in the heart of the marketing district, and retreated to Garroway's and Jonathon's coffee shops. In the eighteenth century Jonathon's burnt down, and a central area for trading in stocks and shares was included in the design of the new building. The proprietor of Jonathon's charged a daily entry fee. The brokers took umbrage. They joined together to build the London Stock Exchange in 1773.

In New York there was a similar history. The Stock Exchange began under a tree in Wall Street, from about 1792 to 1794. ("Wouldn't have been much trading in those New York winters," said the man from public relations, making a joke. The audience chuckled.) Then they moved into Tontine's Coffee Shop at 400 Wall Street. Later it became the official New York Stock Exchange...

"Who do you think you are," sneered Peter Armenio, glaring at her as she knelt, scooping up slips of paper from the floor and shoving them into a rubbish bag she dragged at her side. "You come here to work, not to act as if you know something about the business. Silly woman. Wouldn't know a stock or a share if you tripped on one in the toilet. Wipe your hands on it, in mistake for a paper towel, you would." He paused, "Coming here, outside work hours. Snooping around in the gallery. Sitting in on information sessions with students from the university. Making a joke of it. You're not even fit for cleaning, woman. Not fit for cleaning."

Trembling slightly – whether from apprehension or the fact that her legs were wobbly at bending down, kneeling, for so long, she was not sure – Gena Boccassini stood. Peter Armenio's face grew crimson in its fury. How dare she stand when he was talking to her? Insolent!

That evening, she came home without a job.

Angelina Abelardo had worked at cleaning offices for five years. She had landed the job in the top floors of the AMP Building by chance. Luisa Bezzina had moved in, down the street from her, and they fell into conversation at the fruit shop one day, as they pinched and prodded, tested and tried the tomatoes and grapes and squashes and melons. Luisa had been working at the AMP Building, lower levels, for two years. A vacancy had come on the top floors, and she had grabbed at it. She had a reputation for being a good worker, and it paid off. Excitedly, she told Angelina of the splendours of zipping through the cleaning, with all-carpeted areas, thick floor coverings wall-to-wall, shining new bathroom and sink fixtures, glossy desk and board table tops.

The five top floors were particularly important. This was the hub of the business world, the offices where the deals were made and sealed, every telephone call having a potential for success on a grand scale. Even private telephone calls were regarded in this light by the men who inhabited the five top floors: stupendous achievements should always be theirs; they had fought to rise to the top and, working here at the top of (what was once) the tallest building in Sydney (they still thought of it that way), they had made it. They would keep making it. Success was theirs. Invariably theirs. And (although *they* didn't have to think of it, didn't have to arrange it – an office manager directed someone down the line in the logistics) they had to have top cleaners. And top cleaning.

Nothing could be left smeared. Never a stubbed out cig-
arette – or, more often, cigar – could remain in an ashtray over-
night. Mirrors and windows and desk tops and board tables,
every surface situated anywhere on the five top floors, were to
be polished and buffed and patted and preened until sparkling.
Until the reflection of every man working at the top of the AMP
Building shone out at him, his success doubled, tripled,
quadrupled in the light.

Luisa Bezzina joined Penelope Cugliari, who had cleaned
the offices at the top (as the cleaners on the floors below
referred to them) for a year. A short time later, a sought after
vacancy arose. Angelina Abelardo joined them. And some
months later, Gena Boccassini, dismissed from the Stock Exchange, but her worth recognised by Radivoj Cayhan when he
interviewed for the position, arrived at the top. And with her
coming, the syndicate won Lotto.

A fifth level prize, granted. $1807.61 each. Only. Granted.
But a win nevertheless. They hugged each other in joy. And
began to decide on what they would do, each one with her
windfall.

"He's quite cosy in there, as usual," said Luisa Bezzina, as she
returned from the executive staffroom, her hands now empty.
"Settled down for hours. We won't have any interruptions." The
others nodded.

They walked briskly to their assigned stations. As usual,
they had already done the fifty-first, fifty-second and fifty-third
floors, spinning through the work with an inborn energy and a
desire to get on with the real work. This evening, it was Gena's
turn to set herself up, vacuum and duster at the ready, on the
top floor, in easy view of the executive staffroom. If Radivoj
Cayhan did come out, prowling around the floors, contrary to
his usual habits, she would know immediately. She would be in
a position to phone down to the fifty-first floor, alerting Penelope and Luisa, who were ensconced in alcoves, at secretarial
desks, telephones and computer terminals at hand.

Angelina was taking her turn as lookout on the fiftieth floor,
poised to telephone through a warning if anyone came up from
below. Unusual if they did: the general practice was for the

157

four cleaners assigned to the top floors to work, isolated from the remainder of the building. There was no cause for any of the cleaners or supervisors working on any one of the remaining forty-nine floors to venture up the stairs or the lifts to the upper reaches. "But you never know," said Penelope, when they had first made their plans. "We need a scout to cover Radivoj, and one to be ready in case what never happens, does." It became standard practice to assign two of their number to lookout posts. They took it in turns.

And they took it in turns to telephone through to New York or London, and to collect messages from the fax machine as they came through, spitting out information about the latest share prices in New York, or the ups and downs of the stock market in London.

Sydney, 8.30 PM. London, 2.30 PM. New York, 11.30 AM. It was very easy, when you thought about it. And Luisa Bezzina, Penelope Cugliari, Angelina Abelardo and Gena Boccassini had thought about it. Long.

They had apportioned the $7230.44 Lotto win, mentally sharing it out between the four of them. $1807.61. Not a neat sum. A useful one? Perhaps string it out over the weeks, using it to buy little luxuries for numerous breakfasts and dinners... But the luxuries would come to an end. $7230.44 split four ways wouldn't last long. Maybe put it toward a deposit on a new car. Well, a new second hand car...But it would be a very small deposit, nowadays. Then keep it in the bank. Build on it. Save for something special. But how special? Be saving for years, if it was something each of them *really* wanted. Something expensive. Major...Well, all right. Spend it all. Now. At once. A quarter share would take one person to Noosa and back, with the hire of a yacht tossed in. They could go together. Leave their families behind. Spend two glorious weeks on the sand, lying on the beaches...Losing their jobs! Would Radivoj Cayhan give each of them two weeks off, all at once. All four. Together? It wasn't even a question. They knew the answer without asking it.

Gena Boccassini suggested it. It was so simple. All they needed to do was to establish an account with a New York stockbroker, and a London firm. And right there, on the fifty-third floor of the AMP Building, in a luxurious office with large swivel chair, gargantuan desk, liquor cabinet and two leather couches, Gena found an international business directory. With a section on stockbrokers. Meany and Strange, 300 Wall Street, New York, NY, leapt out of the page. Hutch, Jackson and Towler, London SW1, provided the London end. Good, competent, sturdy sounding names.

Yet neither of them was as impressive as that appearing on their letterhead, the letterhead designed by Angelina, Luisa, Geanette and Penelope, created and printed especially for this new venture: "Abelardo, Bezzina, Boccassini and Cugliari Inc." The address? "AMP Building, Circular Quay, Sydney, Australia." But, more importantly: "Fax (02) 603 4644."

They established accounts with the First International Bank of Detroit and Lloyds of London. Credit? $3615.22 in each. And then they began.

"Metronome Gas and Pipe: Selling – $2.50. Last sale – $2.35; DHS Oil and Shale: Selling – 45 cents. Last sale – 50 cents; Suni Camber: Selling – $1.35. Last sale – $1.00," began the fax that spewed out of the machine and into Luisa Bezzina's hands. She read down the list, her eyes darting from one entry to the next, her mind going back to the list faxed through from London half an hour ago, and the one half an hour before that.

Abelardo, Bezzina, Boccassini and Cugliari Inc. were following the market avidly. They were playing the percentage game, as they say in the business. "Buy in gloom and sell in boom" was the adage they followed: invest in the midst of a bear market, when prices are falling; sell in a raging bull market, when prices are shooting sky high. The knack was to sell just before the price tops, then topples...down to the depths. Or even a slump. Get out just at the right time. And "the firm" studied the fundamentals of the companies in which they invested, or thought to invest. They devised a checklist of risk-inducing pointers, keeping them always to the fore when they decided whether to buy, or whether to sell. They looked at performance factors, financial stability, track record, the distribution of dividends to shareholders, the dividend rate and dividend yield, the companies' earnings per share (dividing a company's net profit by the total number of shares in the company), the price/earnings ratio (the number of times the price of the share covers the earnings per share), the liabilities of the various companies, management objectives, gearing. And they directed their attention not at the blue-chip stocks, the stocks listed on the mainboards at stock exchanges all over the world, the tried and true stocks, the stocks which were seen as rendering solid returns, the best for the sound investor to take up. No, Abelardo, Bezzina, Boccassini and Cugliari, Inc. directed their attention at the medium and smaller industrial companies, the "green chips". They had observed, early on, that these companies performed significantly better than the "blue chips". They were careful. But they were daring. They studied the market. They invested wisely, according to their own sights. They used their good sense of what was running low, what was sailing high, and when the running would stop. And they took chances. Chances based on their knowledge of the market, their study of the trends, of the companies, of the buying and selling that went on, in London, New York, Sydney. Chances which paid off.

"It looks like Metronome's on the way up, Penelope. Get onto Meany's. Tell them we want 15,000 at $2.35, but we'll go to $2.45," she yelled. Penelope, sitting at the desk in the alcove in the corner picked up the phone and dialled New York. The Exchange had just opened. It was 10.00 AM New York time. She put in the order. A pause. Operating on the Computer Assisted Trading System, commonly known in the trade as CATS, the sale was confirmed immediately. Down the line came the message: "Fifteen thousand at $2.37, confirmed." There was a short pause, then Penelope heard her Meany's broker shouting down the line:

"You're on to something, Buzzi's...The next sale...The next sale is at $2.54. They're going up. You've hit the jackpot."

Meany's, familiar now with their longterm customer Abelardo, Bezzina, Boccassini and Cugliari, adopted the American way of friendship to a client from so far away. Around the globe. The otherside of the world. "Buzzi's" had become a trusted client of Meany and Strange, Stockbrokers. All they had had in their Meany's account from the first was $3615.22, on the First National Bank of New York. But had never needed it. Right from the beginning that Downunder bunch had got it right. Making money hand over fist, went the word around Meany's. Golden touch. A canny sense of the market, those Aussies. Funny, never spoke with the men in charge. But the women down the line seemed competent enough. Knew what they were doing. Never a hesitation, never a wrong move. Never a loss.

"Sell. Sell." The firm voice broke in, over the phone, into the brief silence at the New York end. "Off load them at $2.65."

"The whole 15,000?" "The lot." The voice was clear and determined. The man at Meany's obeyed. Fifteen thousand, bought in at $2.37. Sold at $2.65. The difference to be transferred immediately into their First National Bank Account. Confirmation was immediate, through CATS. No need for contract notes, sent through the mail. In these days of automation, the phone was enough. And the fax backed it up. No one in the business used stamps anymore. Or envelopes...

Penelope directed her thanks into the telephone. The man at the other end made a note. She rang off.

At the other end of the office, the fax machine was chattering away. "Mannix Engineering, Inc.: Selling – 62 cents. Last sale – 62 cents. BXR Rayon: Selling – $2.31. Last sale – $2.29..." Luisa walked over to Penelope's desk – well, the AMP desk on the fifty-first floor, commandeered by Abelardo & Co., Inc. where Penelope, or Luisa, or Angelina, or Gena sat, on one or other of the week nights of cleaning. Leaning on the top of the computer display unit, she smiled. "Good enough for one evening's work, Penelope, hey?" "Plus the 10 cents per share on the 20,000 Royal Blues," replied Penelope, thinking back on the night's transactions with the London end. Hutch, Jackson and Towler. Couldn't forget them. Indeed, it was their faxes which often meant the difference between succeeding in New York, or missing out. Though they missed out hardly at all. And had never made a loss.

When London was closing, New York was opening up. When they ran through the final prices from Hutch's, they rang

Meany's, buying at the opening price and selling, whether that day or the next, at a higher closing price. When the shares rose, they sold. When they fell, they hung on to them, getting the sense of the market, and a feel for when they should get out, off load stocks bought on a high. The firm of Abelardo, Bezzina, Boccassini and Cugliari had accounts at Lloyd's and the First National in six figures, now. And still rising. Fast.

Gena keyed in the latest transaction. She ran backwards, over the long list of buys and sells, the figures appearing alongside, recording the fortunes of Abelardo, Bezzina, Boccassini and Cugliari. She pressed "print". Requested four copies. Heard the printer rev itself up. Saw the crisp, white pages spewing forth. (It was the end of the month. Time for an appraisal of their performance. The company's performance.) Then she signed off, keying in the exit word which kept the account sealed, away from the daily transactions recorded in the computer. No chance a day operator could key in to the accounts of Abelardo and Co., Inc. The password? What else but "Moonlighting".

In April 1987 the stockmarket plummeted. Meany's noted that their prize customer, Abelardo, Bezzina, Boccassini and Cugliari, suffered not at all. "Good nose for the market, that lot," they muttered to each other in the offices of Hutch, Jackson and Fowler, London sw1. "Can't fault them Downunder. *Still* making it in the market," went the whisper around Meany and Strange, Stockbrokers.

Tokyo took over from New York as the largest Stock Exchange in the world. Abelardo, Bezzina, Boccassini and Cugliari opened an account with the Bank of Tokyo. The time differential was not so great between Sydney and Tokyo as Sydney and London, and New York. Luisa, Angelina, Gena and Penelope pondered how they would make use of their Tokyo link, in the night hours Sydney time, when they were cleaning, or cleaning up. They had no doubt they would find a way.

SPINIFEX PRESS

is a new independent publishing venture that
publishes innovative and controversial feminist
titles by Australian and international authors.
Our list includes fiction, poetry and non-fiction
across a diverse range of topics with a radical and
optimistic feminist perspective.

*Spinifex Press was awarded the international
Pandora New Venture Award for 1991 from
Women in Publishing (UK).*

OTHER SPINIFEX TITLES

FICTION

Too Rich
by Melissa Chan.
ISBN: 1-875559-02-7

You can never be too thin or too rich,' said Wallis Simpson, Duchess of Windsor. But Francesca Miles, independent feminist detective, disagrees. When one of the richest men in Sydney is found dead in his penthouse she teams up with Inspector Joe Barnaby in a mystery that follows the trials and tribulations of a family that should have everything money can buy.

'...an intelligent and politically interesting plot.'
Venetia Brissenden, *Mean Streets*.

'Hooray for Melissa Chan and may she write many more who-dunnits.'   *WEL-Informed*.

'...an immensely entertaining read'   *Ita*.

FICTION

Angels of Power and other reproductive creations
edited by Susan Hawthorne and Renate Klein
ISBN: 1-875559-00-0

In the tradition of Mary Shelley's *Frankenstein*, the writers in this book use technological developments as their starting point in tracing the consequences of reproductive technologies. Imagination, vision and a good joke come together and demonstrate that women can resist the power of god-like scientists who long to create monsters and angels. With contributions by writers from Australia, New Zealand, Canada and USA.

'*Angels of Power* is an important ground-breaking anthology...'
Karen Lamb, *Age*.

'*Angels of Power* should head the reading list of any course in ethics and reproductive technology.'
Karin Lines, *Editions*.

'...renders ethical issues imaginatively through fiction and contributes significantly to this important debate.'
Irina Dunn, *Sydney Morning Herald*.

FICTION

The Falling Woman
by Susan Hawthorne
ISBN: 1-875559-04-3

The Falling Woman memorably dramatises a desert journey in which two women confront ancient and modern myths, ranging from the Garden of Eden to the mystique of epilepsy, and the mysteries of the universe itself. In the guise of three personae – Stella, Estella, Estelle – the falling woman struggles to find the map for her life and meet the challenge of her own survival.

'This is a beautiful book, written with powerful insight and captivating originality.'   Julia Hancock

POETRY

Sybil: The Glide of Her Tongue
by Gillian Hanscombe
ISBN: 1-875559-05-1

'Gillian Hanscombe performs a feat of lesbian imagination in this stunning sequence. Her sybilic voice, familiar and strange at once, radiates both vision and anger in a prose that echoes the music of our thoughts back to us. Sybil gives us a lesbian erotic, a lesbian politics, a lesbian tradition, grounded in what Suniti Namjoshi defines as the prophetic. Welcome to lesbian imagination singing at full range.'

Daphne Marlatt

'That *Sybil* happily bears comparison with the works of Sappho, Virginia Woolf and Adrienne Rich is, in my view, a measure of just how important this work is to lesbian literature, and *therefore* to literature in general.'   Suniti Namjoshi

'*Sybil: The Glide of Her Tongue* is a prophetic fugue in lesbian past, present and future time, Sybilline tidings of lesbian existence.'   Mary Meigs

'I am enamoured of *Sybil*. Gillian Hanscombe is one of the most insightfully ironic, deliciously lyrical voices we have writing amongst us today.'   Betsy Warland

'A book where the lesbian voice meditates the essential vitality of she dykes who have visions. A book where Gillian Hanscombe's poetry opens up meaning in such a way that it provides for beauty and awareness, for a space where one says yes to a lesbian *we* of awareness.'   Nicole Brossard

NON-FICTION

The Spinifex Book of Women's Answers
by Susan Hawthorne
ISBN: 1-875559-03-5

Who was the first writer in the world? What was the name of the first novel ever published? What was the name of the woman God made before making Eve? Who was the first woman to make a million dollars? Who wrote *The Autobiography of Alice B. Toklas*? Who wrote the first convict novel in Australia? Who invented the wheel? Who did Einstein's mathematics? Who started the Russian Revolution with the cry 'Bread and Roses'?

All were women. When the next person asks you: Where are the famous women painters/architects/composers/writers/scientists? - this book will help you show exactly who many of them were.

'It should be compulsory reading in every Year Ten class.'
Alison Coates

Non-Fiction

RU 486: Misconceptions, Myths and Morals
Renate Klein, Janice G. Raymond and Lynette J. Dumble
ISBN: 1-875559-01-9

A controversial book about the new French abortion pill. The authors examine the medical literature on the drug, including its adverse effects. They evaluate the social, medical and ethical implications, including the use of women for experimental research, in particular third world populations, and the importance of women-controlled abortion clinics. The book is excellent case study material for medical, health and women's studies practitioners and students.

The authors are experts in feminist ethics, women's health and medical science.

Certificate of Commendation, Human Rights Award (non-fiction), 1991.

NON-FICTION

Nothing Mat(t)ers: A Feminist Critique of Postmodernism
by Somer Brodribb
ISBN: 1-875559-07-8

'Postmodernism exults female oblivion and disconnection; it has no model for the acquisition of knowledge, for making connections, for communication, or for becoming global, which feminism has done and will contunue to do.'

In this challenging and controversial work political theorist, Somer Brodribb, explains the foundations of recent theory and criticises the misogynist and patriarchal nature of the work of Jacques Lacan, Michel Foucault, Jacques Derrida, Jean Baudrillard and Jean-Francois Lyotard. Her rigorous scholarship and original readings demystify postmodernism.

Somer Brodribb is a Canadian feminist theorist who works in the Department of Political Science at the University of Victoria, BC, Canada.

'In this eloquent work Somer Brodribb...literally creates a new discourse in feminist theory.'   Kathleen Barry

'This is an iconoclastic work brilliantly undertaken by Somer Brodribb.'   Andrée Michel

'This is a long-awaited and much-needed book from a tough minded...scholar.'   Janice Raymond